# THE BROKEN CHAIN Reaction

## RASHARD ROYSTER

© 2018 Rashard Royster, *The Broken Chain Reaction*

*Unless otherwise indicated any scripture references are taken from the King James Version.*

**Published by Angel B. Inspired Inc.**
Charlotte, NC 27407
www.angelbinspired.com

**ISBN-13: 978-0-9861335-3-4 | ISBN-10: 0-9861335-3-1**


**Assistant Editor**: Broderick James Williams, NC A&T State Univ.

**Cover & Interior Design**: DHBonner Virtual Solutions, LLC.
www.dhbonner.net


**Library of Congress Control Number: 2018933307**

Printed in the United States of America

*This book is dedicated to all of those who want to change their lives and don't know how.*

Delight thyself also in the Lord:
and He shall give thee the desires of thine heart.

**~Psalm 37:4**

# ACKNOWLEDGEMENTS

I would like to take this time to give a special *thank you* to all who have helped me along my journey:

First, I must give thanks to our Lord and Savior, Jesus Christ... Without Him, none of this would be possible.

Second, to my mother, Catherine Weaver who always loved me; never gave up on me... no matter what.

And then, to my beautiful wife, Celena Royster, who stuck by my side through all the ups and downs...

To my publisher, Angel R. Miller (Angel Barrino) of Angel B. Inspired Inc., who brought this book to life... She is a Super Hero, I tell you.  She gave me so much advice and really coached me through this whole process. And, to her graphics team and illustrator, DHBonner Virtual Solutions, thank you for your amazing cover design and contributions to this project.

To my Pastor, Canton Jones, whose words helped mold me into the man you see now.

And last, but not least, to all my supporters who waited so patiently and downloaded the pre-orders, thank you so much.

This has truly been a Blessing. I love you all!

Thanks,

**Rashard "Brother Rizz" Royster**

# INTRODUCTION

What's up readers? My name is Johnathon. At least that s what my Momma put on my Birth Certificate. Everybody calls me JB, short for Jonny boy. A lot of folks say I'm still young because I'm thirty-five, I don't know if I agree or not.

Some days I feel thirty-five, other days I feel like I'm 'bout fifty.

I guess that comes from hanging around the old coons under the tree all the time.

I'm from St. Petersburg FL, what we call "Da Burg." I done seen a lot and did a lot and like most people from "Da Burg" I done had a rough life. You will see that my story takes place in St. Petersburg and there is some action that takes place in surrounding areas such as Lakeland.

A lot of days I sit and think to myself, how did I make it? Then after my thirty second daydream I say thank you Jesus.

Yep, that's how I made it.

It was nobody but God; he can take the worst situation and turn it around. The Lord Jesus Christ did what I thought was impossible. He brought me out of the dark into the marvelous light; he blessed me. My Momma told me one day; she said, *"Baby God blessed you so you could be a blessing to others."*

She was right because now I see others living the same life I once lived and I just want to help them.

So without further delay I would like to share with you a wonderful story. A story of one man who ran into God, got to know God and changed his life.

A person who was freed from the chains that were keeping him from living the life he was born to live. Then that same man who was broken from his chains went on to help another break loose from his chains. Then that person helped another, and another helped another, and another, and another. Ladies and Gentlemen, be prepared to be blessed.

This is...

*The Broken Chain Reaction*

# CHAPTER 1

Music playing and JB attempted to sing along, *"Don't you know we love you, dear Momma? Place no one above you, dear Momma."*

Mike looked at Chris and said, "Hey Chris you hear this fool? All off rhythm trying to sing. Sound like a raccoon with the flu."

Chris humming a tune himself said, "Yeah I hear him, he need to pass dat blunt, pass da blunt dawg you can't smoke and sing. You either inhaling or you wasting weed bro."

Mike said, "Straight up ... let me hit dat."

JB was still singing, *"Lady, don't you know we love you, dear Momma."*

Chris began clowning him, "Alright big possum face sissy, 2Pac gone come get you bout messing up his song. Come on man pass da blunt dang."

JB looked in the mirror and handed the blunt to Chris over his shoulder, "Here nigga, acting like a crack head in the back seat. And for your information 2Pac stole that song from me."

Chris and Mike both laughed at him, "Haaaaaaaa."

JB said, "I wrote Dear Momma boy. I sung that song to my old girl on Mother's Day when I was like 12 and she been wanting me to sing it every year ever since. I be running out of stuff to buy though. I done bought a microwave, a lawn mower and that joker was like $400.00. I done bought a necklace, shoes, purses and balloons."

Mike with his foolishness said, "I bought my Momma a gun."

JB looked at him, "Bro a gun dawg fo real"?

Chris said, "Dats what she wanted."

Mike replied "Yep, she said just in case somebody break into her house she can blow they butt right back out the front door."

JB started laughing, "Boy ya'll know ya'll from the ghetto, this the only fool I know bought they Momma a gun for Mother's Day. Man I'm bout to hit up this Starbucks and get her a $50 gift card so she can drink coffee till she drop, and let her go on this cruise to Mexico."

Chris said, "Boy you stupid I swear. Man, I'll send her to the laundry mat with a roll of quarters and a bucket of super bleach."

JB said "This nigga dumb, boy you bout to make me crash. Where this Starbucks at bro? Ain't it on 4th Street somewhere?"

Mike said, "Yeah it's where all them white people be sitting outside, I think that's 9th avenue north or something."

Chris put his two cents in, "Yep 9th look at this ol' expensive ass nigga buying gift cards for his Mommy. Be drinking left over Folgers out of plastic cups messing round with me."

JB looked in the mirror again at Chris. "Bro why you hate yo Momma so much? She gave birth to yo big headed ass."

"Boy I ain't even gone say nothing."

JB said, "She still gave birth to you."

"Nigga she had a C-section. She was so high she couldn't even push."

Mike clowning Chris said, "That explains why you so retarded."

JB said, "That's it right there. Starbucks, where all the rich folks go. You know I ain't never been inside there?"

Mike replied, "Shih, me neither. You black folks don't hang out at stuff like this. Matter fact I ain't never even heard a black person talk about Starbucks."

Chris replied, "Ummm so tell me again what makes you wanna come here, ain't yo momma black?"

Mike laughing at Chris said, "He got a point, Mr. Funny man actually got a point, and I wanna hear this.'

JB annoyed with both of them said, "I don't know nigga, it's Mother's Day tomorrow I'm just trying to do something special. I know she drink coffee every morning from 7-11. I figured she might wanna try some new Mocha lattes or whatever you call it."

Chris was still clowning JB... "Rich folks, Mocha Latte, frappe fraps, man if McDonald's .99 cent coffee ain't good enough then I don't know what to tell her. This nigga a new age drug dealer. *The Starbucks Dope Man*. Man ... go take your sophisticated criminal ass in there, I'm staying in the car."

JB said, "Yes please, because we don't need the white folks calling the police on a nigga, 'cause I know you gone act stupid."

Mike agreed, "Super stupid."

Chris said, "I ain't fenna go in there."

Mike had a one track mind ... "I bet they got some sexy snow bunnies working behind the counter."

Chris said, "They ain't gonna want your African looking ass."

JB was ready to go inside, "Mike come on dawg, and let's go be the first black niggas from the hood to walk up in Starbucks."

Chris still clowning said, "On the day before Mother's Day two black guys make history by purchasing a $50 gift card. Them fools so high I bet they gone come out with two large cups and a pack of sugar that's it."

DING ... the door opened ... JB and Mike were greeted by the Starbucks cashier, "*Welcome to Starbucks.*"

JB responded back, "Hey what's up?"

JB and Mike walked up to the counter. The cashier greeted them again, "How are you doing today and how may I help you?"

JB looked at her and said, "Ummm ya'll sell gift cards right?" JB looked at her name tag. "Oh, my bad, how you doing Erica?"

"She black," says Chris as he magically appears out of nowhere.

JB said, "Oh boy here we go, dawg don't start please."

"I'm sorry Mrs."

Erica laughs. "That's alright, I see he didn't pay attention in school, I'm actually Brown not Black." She says with a smile on her face.

Chris feeling silly said, "Oh she got jokes huh?"

"No, no, no dawg, you straight, zip it Chris, zip it."

"To answer your question sir, yes we do have gift cards. We have $10, $25, $50 & $100. Would you like to purchase one?"

"Yeah let me get that $50 card."

"Ok that'll be $53.21." Chris said, "Tell me how you gone buy a $50 gift card and it come up to $53? Starbucks raping people."

JB & Mike both shook their heads and Erica smiled.

Chris feeling himself said, "Hey, Erica you pretty do you have a boyfriend baby?"

"Thank you sir and no I don't."

JB interrupted, "Would you please leave this woman alone Chris? She don't wanna be your lady or go on no kind of dates with you."

Chris said, "How you know nigga, I look better than yo African looking ass."

Erica laughed again. "See I make her laugh."

Mike chimed in, "Nigga you make everybody laugh. You a class clown. Should've been a damn comedian somewhere, but not in Starbucks so shut up."

Erica handed JB the gift card, "There you go sir, thank you and have a nice day, please come again."

JB responded, "Okay you too, and happy early Mother's Day."

"Thank you but I'm not a Mother."

"Oh my bad, well … have a good day anyway."

Chris still full of himself said, "Hey Erica can I get your number sugar?"

Erica smiled. "I'm sorry but no thank you."

They all walked out of the store and back to the car. Mike said, "Nigga you a fool, why you messing with that girl? I thought you were staying in the car anyway."

JB laughed, "This nigga popped up out of nowhere like the damn state farm insurance man." "Oh like a good neighbor State Farm is there ass nigga."

Mike shook his head, "Talking bout she black. She was sexy though."

JB agreed, "Yes she is."

Mike looked at JB and said, "Hey ain't you suppose to get a bag or something, you gonna give your Momma the card just like that?"

JB said, "Oh snap good thinking." JB threw the keys to Mike. "Here start the car let me run back in there right quick."

JB went back inside. "Excuse me pretty but do you have the bag this card comes in?"

Erica responded, "No sir we don't carry the bags, but there is a CVS right across the street. They should have some for a couple of dollars, try them."

"Appreciate it Mrs. Erica; you so sweet. I'm surprised you ain't got no man. You should let me take you out some time."

"Thank you but ummm, you're really not my type. I'm sorry I don't mean to be rude."

"Wow! Hmmm that's cool, I'm just saying though, you don't even know me. How can you say that? Unless you saying I don't look like your type. If you are saying that then that would be judging. I know you heard the saying never judge a book by its cover. I'm a cool dude sweetie."

Erica was very observant. She responded, "A cool dude that smells like weed."

Meanwhile back in the car Mike & Chris were talking. Chris said, "You know that nigga in there trying to get that number."

Mike responded, "You already know, it don't take that long to get no bag."

Chris said, "She stuck up, she ain't gone give it to him ... watch. Man where that blunt at? Fire it up."

Back inside the Starbucks JB was still trying to get Erica's number.

She said, "I never said you weren't cool or anything."

JB interrupted her, "You just saying what exactly? You look at my friends and think what? You see me and think what? I guarantee if we go out one time I can change the way you think about me. Just one time, tomorrow. Just because you ain't no mother doesn't mean you can't have a good time and be treated nice, there is no holiday for that."

Erica asked JB a question that threw him off guard "What's your relationship with GOD like?"

JB found himself in a spot he had never been in before. No girl he had ever been with asked him about GOD. He had been to church as a kid with his Grandmother but as an adult that was one place he wasn't familiar with. He knew that the wrong answer could kill his chances and waiting too long to answer could also, so he came up with a speedy lie. Anything to get her from behind that counter into his reach.

"My relationship with GOD is excellent. Matter of fact that'll give us something to talk about tomorrow."

"You're a smooth talker, I think I might just have to take you up on that offer just to see if it's legit."

He was thinking, *oh my GOD what have I done,* but that thought was quickly replaced by *well at least I got her.*

She said, "You could be a con artist."

"Yeah right, a con artist hanging out with that fool in the car."

She laughed and said, "Yes he is a hand full."

"Okay so listen, they probably thinking something by now so let me get your number, so I can get back out there. I know you don't want him coming back in here."

She responded, "No you're right, let him stay out there, but I'm still not giving you my number. If you want to take me out you can meet me here tomorrow at 9:00 pm. Is that good enough for you sir? Mr. I'm waiting on a name."

"Oh yeah sorry, my name is JB. That's cool I'll be here at 8:45 sweetie."

"Okay Mr. JB we'll see."

Chris was still running his mouth, "Boy this nigga in there probably in there singing to her, you know he always thinking he Gerald Levert."

Mike responded, "Yeah he done been in there a lil too long."

Chris shook his head … "He probably had to go to the bathroom. Girls don't like it when you first meet them and you gotta do number two around them. Hell I don't like it when they gotta do number two around me. Boy it ain't nothing worse than when a girl blow up the bathroom."

Mike replied, "I swear, especially if they sexy. Oh there he go right there. Let me hit that before he get in here."

JB opened the car door.

Chris said, "This nigga was in there 'bout twenty minutes and still ain't get no bag, boy you good, you gotta teach me that trick."

Mike cosigned, "I'm telling ya." Mike tapped Chris on the arm and pointed at JB. "What the hell was taking so long?"

Chris clowned him, "Yeah JB, I hope you wasn't in there on one knee asking that girl to marry you." Chris tapped Mike back on the arm and laughed. "She might be black or brown or whatever she is, that don't mean she like brownish black niggas. I wonder what school she went to talking bout I ain't pay attention. All my life we been Black, now all of a sudden we Brown."

Mike laughed, "She was being funny fool."

Chris said "She ain't funny, I can show her how to be funny."

JB interrupted, "Okay Chris get your mind right." He said, "Boy for one I was only in there for two minutes maybe three, and that's because the line was long."

Chris said, "But you still ain't get no bag."

"That's because they ain't have no bags Mr. Funny man. Oh brown ass, we gone start calling you Chris Brown. They don't carry bags I gotta go to CVS, man let me hit that blunt."

Chris changed the subject, "I ain't gone lie that coffee was smelling good as hell."

Mike and JB chimed in together "Fo real!"

The boys went to CVS then made their way back to the hood.

* * *

*The Next Day*

JB pulled up to his Mother's house and got out of the car. An old man named Rufus who JB knew since he was a kid yelled from across the street.

Mr. Rufus yelled out, "Hey *John-John*, boy that's a sharp car you got there. You gotta let an old man like me take it for a spin one day. I can get some honeys in a car like that. You take my Ford and let me take that. Ha, ha."

"Naw Mr. Ru I don't think your wife would like you riding around town with five women in the car. Can you handle five of them Mr. Ru?"

"Oh yeah, back in my days . . ."

JB cut him off, "There go yo wife right there."

Mr. Rufus turned quick to see if she was listening, and JB laughed.

"Yeah you ain't got it no more Mr. Ru, you retired from the game. Mrs. Simpson will kick you up and down this street if she see you with a young girl."

"Yeah you right *John-John* we done been married 57 years. Them girls nice to play with but ain't nothing like having a wife son. Proverbs 18:22 says, 'he who finds a wife finds a good thing. And obtains favor from the Lord.' You ever thought about getting married *John-John*?'"

"Who me? Heck Naw, not right now. I'm too young for all that. Plus these lil heffas out here ain't bout nothing, I knock them off and send them down the road. They ain't no good Ru, they just want money."

"You just going after the wrong ones that's all. What you need is you an old nice church girl. A church woman will change your life, my wife changed mine."

JB looked at his watch. "I hear you Mr. Ru, hey matter of fact I got a date with a church girl tonight. But first I gotta get in here and holler at my Momma right quick. I'll catch you next time Mr. Ru."

"Ok John-John and tell Cynt I said, 'Happy Mother's Day.'"

JB yelled back as he knocked on the door. "Alright . . ."

"Momma open this door, it's hot out here."

"Who is it, knocking and banging like the police?"

"It's me Ma." The door opened and JB was standing there with balloons, flowers and a teddy bear. He yelled with a big smile on his face ... *"Happy Mother's day Ma."*

Then he started to sing, *"Don't you know I love you, dear Momma? Place no one above you, dear Momma."*

"Aww thank you son, I wasn't expecting you to come over this early. I was just making me some coffee and 'bout to cook breakfast. Come in before them nasty flies get in my house. What you doing up so early?"

"Oh I had something to do this morning. Speaking of coffee though, why don't you open up this bag and see what you got." He handed her the bag with the Starbucks gift card inside.

"What's this son? It's too small and too light to be a coffee maker. Oh what's this? A $50 gift card from

Starbucks. Boy who fenna go down there and drink those White folks coffee? You always trying to surprise me. Well you show got me this time. I never been down there."

"It's nice and clean in there Ma, and they be having that coffee smelling good up in there."

"I guess, if you say so I don't know nobody who drink Starbucks boy." She laughed. "But thank you son at least you tried."

"You welcome Ma, just look at it like this, you don't know nobody in Mexico either. So get ready because you 'bout to drink strange coffee around a bunch of strange strangers."

Cynt looked confused. "Huh?"

"Yeah Ma." He handed her two plane tickets to Mexico along with a hotel brochure. "You going to Mexico."

He noticed that there was a puzzled look on her face so he said it a second time. This time like the price is right game show host. "You're going to Mexico, 5 days 4 nights in a tropical suite drinking Starbucks the whole time."

She jumped up and hugged him. "Boy, you always do good things for your momma. Thank you, son. I love you so much."

She wiped the tears running down her face. "God bless you baby. Oh Jesus I don't know what I'm going to wear to Mexico. And you got two tickets too, I guess I can take your crazy behind auntie with me. Oh my God thank you so much Johnathan.

So what you got planned today?"

"Oh nothing really, you know chill in the hood but tonight . . ."

She cut him off, "Now Johnathan I done told you over and over about hanging in them streets, you know I don't like you doing all that mess. Especially hanging around them thugs you wanna call your friends. I hate to say it but they gone get you in trouble son. Every time I turn around Sophia calling me. Her boy's in jail, they done got in a fight and somebody was shooting behind her house. You better not have nobody coming around here shooting up my house. Or you can buy yourself a plane ticket to Mexico because I'm gone kill you. You hear me boy?"

"Yes ma'am." "And you can wipe that smile off your face 'cause it ain't funny. You use to be a nice boy, now you all out there selling drugs and GOD knows what else. That's what you need too."

"What?"

"Some GOD boy. You use to go to church every Sunday with your Grandma, now you act like you don't know who Jesus is. All ya'll, all yo lil' friends need to go to church. Around here chasing these lil' stank girls, you gone mess around and catch something."

"Naw as a matter of fact that's what I was about to say. I met a church girl, yesterday at Starbucks, that's who sold me the card. We going out tonight."

"Oh Lord, I hope you don't go around that girl smelling like weed and liquor. Take your momma advice. Them lil' chicks you talk to might like it because they smoke it with you but a church girl ain't gone give you the time of day smelling and looking all messed up. A real woman like a clean cut man that look like he got something going for himself."

JB had never seen his Father before and very seldom heard stories about him, so every once in a while he would ask a question about his dad. "So when you first met my dad what was he like?"

"Boy look at me, I wasn't always like this. I was wild when I met your daddy, and he was wild too, and that's what I liked at that time. But now a days things are different. People grow up and get smarter, or grow up and get dumber. You see he ain't around don't you, you don't ever want to be like him."

"You gotta make sure when you find a woman, a real one, you stay by her side especially if you mess around and get her pregnant. If you say this female a church girl and she agreed to go out with you, she must like you. So that mean don't mess it up. She can like you today ... don't mean she gone like you tomorrow. She ain't one of them girls you get by flashing yo money around like you be doing. You're a handsome young man Johnathon, and you got a good heart. You deserve a nice girl with some morals, what's her name?"

'Erica, and she so sexy too."

She shook her head. "See that's what's gone turn her off right there."

"What?"

"Jonathan, son ... Please don't go around that girl telling her how fine she looks. I mean you can say you looking nice tonight. But all that damn girl you fine as hell crap, don't do it or the next time you walk up in Starbucks she gone act like she don't even know you. I'm telling you son, ya'll young men got a lot to learn about women. Everything ain't always about looks or sex. Get to know the girl, talk. That's all you need to be worrying about. Especially on the first date. Talk that's it. The first date, second date, and the third date. Talk, talk, talk and listen. Women like when a man can listen. Always be truthful too; you don't wanna get caught in a lie. If you be upfront in the beginning then there's nothing she can hold against you. If she still wants to see you again after that then she really likes you. I can't tell you how many guys I went out with and never called they butt again. Once girls get turned off it's hard to turn them back on. How old is she?"

"I don't know, I didn't get a chance to ask her all that 'cause I was in line. She look like she 'bout 25 or something."

"Where ya'll going? Have you thought about that yet? About where you wanna take her?"

"Not yet."

"I suggest a nice lil restaurant on the beach somewhere. One that plays a little soft music, like jazz the first impression is the most important baby. You might wanna buy her some flowers and open the doors for her, let her see more than what she probably already thinks you are."

"Dang Momma you trying to make me go all out."

'Go all where? Boy flowers ain't nothing. They won't cost you nothing but $20 and you can get a good dinner for under $60 'cause a Church girl ain't gone order no alcohol. You don't want to either, just play it cool on the first date. Just know that opening doors don't cost you nothing but can get you a lot. Take it from an old woman. You might can spend $10 on a hood rat but I wouldn't advise it. Plus if you can afford Mexico I know you ain't broke boy, not with that nice car you got out there."

"Alright Ma you done took me to date school. We gone see how it goes tonight, and I will let you know in the morning."

"Yes let me know, hopefully she can put some Jesus in yo life boy," she said with a smile.

JB smiled back and reached in for a hug. "Ok Momma I'll talk to you later, I love you."

"I love you too baby."

JB walked out the door and went to his car.

His mom prayed a quick prayer ... "*Lord please let this girl be the one to turn my son around. You know more than anyone that he needs it.*"

# CHAPTER 2

———— ‹◇› ————

JB left his mother's house and went back to the block to meet up with Mike & Chris. They were standing on the block with the rest of the crew. Alvin, Chaz, Bruce, Bam and the twins Rhino & Hippo.

Chaz sounded annoyed, "Man my baby mama talking bout she wanna go to the mall and go shopping for Mother's Day. Who she think she is? I ain't fenna spend all my hard earned money on her. She ain't my lady."

Alvin looked at him and said, "Man, she is yo baby mama though."

Chaz said, "Bro listen, I ain't on that. I'll buy her butt a card from the dollar store."

Mike chimed in "Fool you sound like Chris now, matter of fact where that nigga at?"

Rhino said, "He still sleep. You know that fool ain't fenna be up this early after last night. That nigga was so drunk."

Mike replied, "Yeah but ya'll two niggas like 400 pounds. It take a lot for ya'll, Chris probably weigh a buck and a half soaking wet."

The music was playing loud as JB turned the corner.

Hippo said, "There go JB. Dang we could've told him to bring the cards; if we knew he was coming. Sam and Bruce is taking forever."

Mike replied, "That's 'cause they ain't go through the cut. They went around the block, you know Sam be trying to see if that girl be standing on the porch."

Chaz said, "That nigga still trying to get that lil girl; he gone go to jail messing with that lil girl."

Mike responded, "What she bout seventeen … eighteen?"

Hippo said, "Nah bro she just look like that. Crystal told me chic like 23 and she got two kids.

JB walked up, "Who got two kids?"

Hippo said, "The thick red girl around the corner that stay in that blue house."

JB said, "Oh ... Candice? I just smashed her last week, that booty so soft too."

Mike said, "That nigga don't be playing boy!"

JB changed the subject, "Hey guess who I seen when I rode pass the store?"

Everybody asked, "Who?"

JB said, "That sucker nigga who was running his mouth last night at the club. Talking 'bout we don't get no money and he this and he that."

Alvin said, "Man you talking 'bout that square ass nigga Todd from cross?"

Mike chimed in, "Bruce and Sam probably up there right now. If they see that nigga up there its fenna go down. Hey somebody call Bruce phone, hurry up."

JB called Bruce. "Man it's just ringing. He ain't answering; it went to voicemail. Hold up let me call Sam."

A couple seconds went by in silence.

JB said, "That nigga ain't answering either. Man let's ride up there. Ya'll got ya'll straps?"

Everybody answered at the same time, "Yep, yep you know it."

The boys jumped in JB's car and Hippo and Rhino took off in their car. They arrived at the store and just as they expected, Bruce and Sam were fighting.

His tires were screeching as JB spun into the parking lot with Rhino and Hippo right behind him. JB saw that his friends were outnumbered 4 to 2, so he and the crew jumped in. A crowd gathered around, while people were screaming, and others took out their phones to get the fight on video.

It was total chaos in front of the store.

One of the guys from the other crew hit Sam in the head with a bottle and knocked him out unconscious. Hippo spotted one of the men trying to make a run for the trunk of his car, so he pulled out his gun and started shooting.

Alvin and Chaz had one guy cornered by the ice machine. They were beating him bad, he was leaking blood everywhere. Rhino picked up Sam off the ground and drug him to the car; he was still dizzy from the blow to the head.

Meanwhile Mike fought with one guy and Bruce with another. The guy who made a run for the trunk never made it. Hippo shot him twice in the chest and once in the leg.

The crowd scattered.

JB panicking said, "Come on man let's go, everybody let's go."

Bruce yelled at Hippo, "Man get in the car let's go nigga."

Mike yelled, "The camera, the camera ... hold on I got to get the tape man."

Meanwhile one of the other guys took off for the trunk and pulled out an AK 47. Alvin yelled, "That nigga got a chopper."

Hippo began shooting again.

Alvin pulled out his gun and started shooting and so did Chaz. JB put his car in reverse and backed up so fast he didn't take time to see who was behind him and before he knew it he ran over Bruce's leg who was trying to get in the back seat.

They heard the sirens; the police were on the way.

31

Mike was in the store screaming at the man behind the counter, "Where the tape? Let me get the video Ali."

But Ali refused to give him the tape.

Mike thought about jumping over the counter to take it, but he thought again. He didn't have enough time, the police would be there in a second, plus being charged with robbery wouldn't look good on his record. Since he already had two strikes he ran out the back door to avoid being shot by the dude outside with the AK 47.

Bruce was screaming and in a world of pain yet managed to hobble his way into the car as JB stopped. JB asked, "Aww man you okay dawg? My bad bro. Man I swear I'm fenna kill them niggas. All those niggas."

In a matter of seconds, the store parking lot was empty, and the boys were speeding down the road. JB asked Bruce, "Yo leg broke dawg? I'm fenna drop you off at the hospital."

Alvin told JB, "Man you know the police fenna come to the hospital."

Bruce screamed, "Man I don't care who at the hospital bro drop me off and keep going. They can't do nothing but get me for fighting. I gotta get my leg locked at, this shit hurt nigga."

JB turned to Chaz and said, "How about you bro? You wanna go too?"

"Naw I just need a big blunt and some Hennessey I'll be straight, we can't go back to the block right now either."

JB was pissed by now, "Damn man! Hey call Hippo and see where them niggas went."

Alvin responded, "I wonder if Mike got that tape because if the police get it Hippo gone. I think he shot that one nigga."

Chaz said, "Yeah he did, bust him a couple times."

JB was hot, "And I'm fenna finish shooting them. They better not let me see them nowhere."

JB's phone rang. JB looked down at the phone and said, "This Mike right here." He answered, "Mike, where you at boy?"

*"I'm on the block where ya'll at?"*

JB responded, "Man you better get off the block, you know that thing fenna be swarming with troll in a minute. I'm dropping Bruce off at Bay Front. Man I was backing up trying to get out of there and done messed around and ran this man leg over."

Mike shook his head and said, *"Damn."*

JB repeated himself, "Hey man get off the block, get somewhere and call me. I'm fenna drop Bruce off and go switch cars."

Meanwhile Alvin called Hippo.

Hippo answered, *"Hello."*

Alvin said, "Where you at bro?"

Hippo sounded scared... *"Man I'm fenna hit it ... I'm out of here. I'm fenna go to ATL. Bro I swear I shot that nigga like four times I think, where ya'll at?"*

Alvin replied, "On our way to Bayfront, JB ran over Bruce and broke his leg.

Hippo replied, *"Damn dawg, what about Chaz?"*

Alvin said, "Oh he straight he say he just wanna get high and drunk."

JB pulled up to the hospital and told Al to go get Bruce a wheelchair, "Hurry up ... be quick we gotta slide." "Damn dawg my bad, go on in there and let them fix you up. Bruce you good bro, we all was trying to get out of there. I rather get my leg broke than to get hit with that big ass choppa that nigga had."

Chaz chimed in, "For real."

JB said, "Hey just don't say nothing when the police come, 'cause I know they coming. A nigga gone have to get a lawyer."

Bruce told him, "Bro you already know I ain't fenna say a word. I hope they knock my ass out with some medicine, this shit hurt. Alright ya'll I'll holla, ya'll boys be safe."

JB pulled off quickly and said, "Damn where we gone go now? Can't go back to the block, I need to make some money too. I was supposed to have a date tonight damn."

Alvin told him, "You might as well go still, you sho can't stay round here till everything die down."

JB knew that when the police looked at the video they would be searching for a blue Jaguar with chrome rims, so he went home to park his car in his garage and switch into his Lexus.

From St. Petersburg to Lakeland, throughout other parts of Florida, Georgia and even North Carolina authorities were placed on alert for everyone involved in the shooting. Lakeland was one of JB's frequent hang outs and he had quite a few customers there, but

St. Petersburg was his main spot. He had to be invisible for a while. The hood remained hot and people asked lots of questions.

JB was anxious about the days to come.

Mike called Chris. He said to himself, *Nigga answer this phone. He can't still be sleep.*

Chris answered in a sleepy voice. *"What up nigga?"*

"What up? We just got in a shootout with that punk ass nigga from the club last night up at the store."

Chris jumped up out of the bed and said, *"I swear I heard some gun shots but I went back to sleep. This was just now?"*

"Yeah nigga about fifteen minutes ago I'm fenna come to your house. The block fenna be hot for a minute."

*"Ok, come on I'm 'bout to get up right now."*

"Bet."

Mike hung up the phone and ten minutes later knocked on Chris' door. Chris came to the door in his boxers. "What's up, what happened?"

"Nigga I thought you was getting up."

Chris still half sleep said, "Nigga I did get up I just didn't put on no clothes. This my house I can walk round butt naked if I want, you got a blunt?"

"Naw."

Chris said, "Fool didn't you just leave the store?"

"And nigga didn't I just tell you we fought them niggas and had a shootout? Hippo shot one of the niggas like five times. Last thing on my mind was a blunt I was trying to get out of there."

"Damn you ain't say ya'll was fighting too, you said shootout I was thinking bang ... bang that's it. What happened?"

"Man I'm trying to tell you if you shut up for a minute."

"Okay go head."

"We was on the block about to gamble but we ain't have no cards, so Bruce and Sam walked to the store. They was gone bout ten minutes then JB came round the corner and said he saw that nigga Todd from the club last night, at the store. So, we was like oh shit Bruce & Sam just went up there, so we called their phones. They ain't answer so we hopped in the whip and flew up there. Show nuff soon as we got there they was already fighting.

It was four niggas jumping Bruce and Sam. We pulled up, hopped out and started getting on them niggas ass. One of the niggas hit Sam cross the head with a bottle and knocked him out. Then one of them tried to go to the trunk and that's when Hippo started busting and hit dude over and over till he fell.

That's when everybody started running.

Well especially when the other nigga made it to the trunk and pulled out a choppa."

Chris just shook his head, "Damn."

"Yeah but before he could shoot it JB, Alvin, Hippo and Rhino pulled out and started busting at him. I was trying to go in the store and get the tape because I already knew troll was gone be on the way. Ali wouldn't give it to me though, so I ran out the back door."

Chris puzzled said, "Why you ran out the back?"

"Because everybody left me and that nigga was still out there with that chopper. If I would've ran out there I would be dead."

"Damn bro."

"Yeah then I guess when they was leaving Bruce fell and JB ran over his leg. Man shit crazy, that junk happened so fast. It just goes to show you boy this street life ain't no joke, one minute you can be chilling about to play cards, five minutes later you can be dead just like that."

Chris still blown away by everything Mike told him said. "Dang Hip, Hip done bust a nigga. Oh snap! If the police get that tape he gone. Boy that's attempted murder."

Chris and Mike both shook their head.

Mike said, "Yep, just like that, young nigga. Man fenna call lil bro and see where he at."

The phone rang but Hippo didn't answer it, he turned his phone off. "Damn lil bro ain't even answer his phone. Man, I need to smoke, damn I can't believe this shit, on Mother's Day too."

Chris said, "Let me call JB and see where he at."

The phone rang and JB answered. "What up boy you done got up huh? You must have already heard."

"JB man you already know, I'm sitting at the crib with Mike right now. He just told me everything, man shit wild. Where ya'll at?"

JB said, "Man I dropped everybody off, I'm fenna go clear my head for a second. Everybody need to split up for about two or three days and don't say nothing to nobody about nothing, to nobody."

Chris said, "Yeah I feel you."

JB was serious, "I'm for real Chris I ain't joking bro, and I know how you like to run your mouth."

"Okay man I ain't fenna say nothing."

"Alright, did Mike get the tape? I forgot to ask him."

"Naw Ali wouldn't give it to him."

"Damn I gotta get a lawyer. Man tell Mike I'll holla at him, ya'll boys be easy."

Chris said, "Yeah alright bro" and hung up the phone. He looked at Mike and said, "Damn that nigga say he fenna lay low for about three days. Say all ya'll need to split up and don't say nothing to nobody."

"I know I ain't gone say nothing. But I'm straight anyway, I ain't shoot all I did was fight. Matter of fact you wasn't even there so you straight too. Go up there and grab some blunts and see what the police talking 'bout. See if they looking at that tape."

Meanwhile JB's moms called him. "Hey Ma what's up?"

'Didn't we just have a long talk this morning about you being in the streets and hanging with them boys?"

"What you talking 'bout Ma?"

"Boy don't even try to play me like I was born yesterday. Sophia just called me talking about its 100 polices at the store and you and them two bad ass twins she got and Lord knows who else, was up there fighting and shooting."

She started crying.

"I hate when you be so hardheaded boy. Every time I hear a gunshot I think somebody gone call my phone telling me my son dead. On Mother's Day Jonathan? Mother's Day? No mother in the world want to hear that her child is dead on Mother's Day, or any other day. You must don't care whether you live or die. Boy do you hear me talking to you?" She spoke in a loud and stern voice.

"Yes Ma I hear you."

"Boy don't you raise your voice at me."

"I ain't raise my voice Ma."

"And don't be talking back either. You gone respect me boy. I don't care how old you get, how much money you can make or how many damn trips to Mexico you buy. You ain't never gone be old enough to disrespect me. You hear me Jonathan Damien Griffin?"

"Yes ma'am."

"Now what happened up there?"

"Four dudes was jumping on Bruce and Sam."

Cynthia was very angry and disappointed with him. She said, "And you want to be a hero in somebody else problem. You think them fools gone help you if you in trouble?"

"Yeah I know they would."

"Whatever boy, do you think they gone take a bullet and die for you? You better get your act right boy. I don't know what's wrong with your generation. Ya'll be fighting, killing and carrying on for no reason. You might as well had of brought me a black dress for Mother's Day if you gone mess around and get killed because somebody else was fighting.

42

They wasn't even fighting you, how stupid can you be? You know everybody know ya'll so they gone tell on you. You ain't gone get away with it. They told Sophia soon as it happened and she called me two minutes later. They say it was one of her sons that killed one of the boys."

"Ma... Ain't nobody get killed they jump in the car and left."

"Boy that's what I'm saying, you think you know everything. He ain't die at the store he died at the hospital."

"How you know Ma?"

"Boy you live in the hood everybody know. All people do is talk, it's all over Facebook and everything. That s why I said I already knew, I was just waiting for you to lie to me. The police gone be coming to knock on my door any minute.

I already know that too, I'll be surprised if they don't. Ain't no use of running you might as well turn yourself in. Just make it easier. And you just met a nice girl, see God tries to bless you and you block it by doing something stupid. Don't go and drag that girl into this mess of yours, I'm telling you she don't deserve it. Maybe you ain't ready to live a grown up life yet. I thought you was but you're not."

"Yes, I am; I just messed up."

"No, you not if you is... prove it. Go and let that girl live her life, you turn yourself in, leave them boys alone, selling drugs and get a real job. When you show me you can do all that then I'll believe you. I got to go I'll talk to you later, you got my blood pressure up."

"Okay I love you Ma."

"Uh huh, bye boy."

After talking to his Mom JB took the battery out of his phone. He didn't want to talk to anyone about anything. He decided that to get his mind off everything we was going to stick to his plans and go on his date with Erica.

# CHAPTER 3

———————◇———————

It was 8:00 p.m. and the sun had just gone down. JB still had not put the battery back in his phone and he wasn't going to. He figured his Mom had probably called him 100 times to see if he was okay or if he was in jail. That wasn't enough for him though, he was too paranoid to talk to anyone, and he wasn't taking any chances.

He had been to the Barber shop, the mall, the carwash, smoked a blunt, had a drink and still there was nothing that could ease his mind and make him stop thinking about what took place earlier.

He even went to the beach to find a nice restaurant for him and Erica, he also bought flowers like his Mom had suggested.

With still one more hour to go before Erica got off he decided to just go to the Starbucks and wait in the parking lot. He backed up in the furthest spot from the building, set his watch alarm for 8:45, laid his seat back and went to sleep.

At 8:45 JB's alarm went off ... Beep ... Beep ... Beep ... Beep ... Beep ... Beep ...

JB jumped up looking around like the police had him surrounded. He forgot that he was at Starbucks. He checked himself out in the mirror, sprayed on a couple squirts of his Polo cologne and gargled a shot of mouth wash.

A couple seconds later he opened the door, spit out the mouth wash and walked across the parking lot.

Once he got inside, he stood there for a minute looking for the sign that said restrooms so he could get one last look at himself; like his mother told him the first impression is the most important. That's when he said to himself, *she already saw me when I came in to buy the gift card. Then she saw me again when I came back in to get the bag. The first impression is way over, this is the 3rd, man I'm wasting my time.*

Then out of nowhere he heard a soft voice behind him.

"So you're the new security guard huh?"

JB turned around and could not believe what he was seeing. This was not the same girl from behind the counter he had met just a day before. This was a woman who looked as if she just stepped off the page of a magazine. She had her hair done, eye lashes bloomed out, lip stick on, sparkling heels and a red carpet dress you would see Halle Berry wearing at the Grammy's.

She was glowing from head to toe.

JB said the first thing that came to mind.

"Will you marry me?" He looked at her to see her response and she looked at him to see if he was serious. After about two seconds they both laughed. "No I'm just kidding, but I must say that you look so, so ... pretty ... more than beautiful. You look like a totally different person."

Erica instantly grew a blushing smile on her face. "Really you think so? Thank you so much, but let's get out of here before my manager comes and tries to talk to me."

She walked out of the store in a hurry.

JB looked around to see if he saw a manager coming and he quickly walked out behind her.

"So you really think I look nice? I didn't know if the dress was too much or not. These heels might be though right? I hope I didn't overdo it. We're not going bowling are we? Because then I would feel stupid."

"What? No. Calm down the dress is not too much. If anything you're too much. You could've wore the Starbucks outfit and that would've been good enough for me."

Erica laughed.

"Don't worry about nothing we definitely are not going bowling, let's go. I hope you don't mind walking in those things because I parked over there."

He pointed to the only car sitting all alone in the far right corner. If you want I can go get it and come back for you.

"No that's okay I can walk."

"Okay, let's go." He extended out his arm to help her off the curve.

"Awe you're such a sweetheart, you didn't have to do that."

"Well I can't let you fall, cause if you do that then I will have to give you mouth to mouth, and then you gone think I'm trying to kiss you."

Erica smiled. "You're funny, I swear I would be so embarrassed if I fell."

"I will catch you."

"Why are you parked way over here anyway?"

"Well for one people can't drive, I don't need nobody running into my car."

"Yes that's a nice car, Lexus. I like it, I see you have good taste. Oh I'm so sorry, speaking of taste I like your outfit and shoes. I meant to tell you that. You look really nice and you smell nice too, what is that you have on?"

"Thank you it's Polo Sport. I couldn't come half stepping I had to get fresh for you." JB hurried in front of Erica, pushed the unlock button on his key chain and grabbed the passenger side door handle. "Let me get that for you your highness."

Erica blushed. "Boy you are too much, I think I like it though. So far so good."

"You think you like it, cool. I know I like it." He quickly walked around to the other side and got in. "So I hope you're hungry because I am."

Erica said, "Yes I'm starving."

"Good well let's go eat."

JB started to turn on the music but thought to himself, "This is a church girl, she doesn't want to listen to TI."

He had to think of something quick because riding without music means silence and silence means awkward moments and awkward moments turn pretty girls like Erica off.

He wasted no time he sprang into action.

"So you're a church girl huh? How long you been going to church?"

"All my life, ever since I could remember. My Grandpa is the Pastor so it's like no getting around it. My whole family goes there. So that's pretty much all I ever known since a little girl."

"And how old are you?"

"I'll be twenty-six in September."

"Oh yeah?"

"Yep, how old are you? Hold up let me guess, twenty-eight or twenty-nine."

JB smiled. "Wrong."

"What, okay twenty-seven, I know you gotta be older me."

"Wrong again, yeah I'm older than you but you still wrong. And how you know I'm older, what makes you think that?"

"Because you act older. You don't act like a lil boy. Like your friend who came by yesterday."

They both laughed.

"Talking bout she black."

They both laughed again.

"Yeah that's my dawg Chris. He cool though, he just a comedian. He always been like that. But to answer your question I'm 32."

"Wow! I never would have guessed that. You definitely don't look 32."

"Thank you."

"You're welcome, do you have any kids Jonathan?"

"Naw I had, well was going to have twins but the girl I was with at the time had a miscarriage at five months."

"I'm so sorry to hear that."

"It's alright."

"So what happened to her? Why are you two not together if you don't mind me asking? Ya'll didn't try again?"

"Well, I was going to but we was always fighting anyways; breaking up and getting back together. I guess GOD knew she wasn't the one for me. The last time we broke up we just never got back together."

"Excuse me, but I gotta ask, you said maybe GOD knew she wasn't the one. You sure it wasn't your fault? I mean you're not crazy are you? You don't have a bad attitude and like to hit women do you?"

JB laughed, "Really? Do I look crazy? Naw I don't beat women sweetie."

"I just had to ask because you never know."

"I ain't got time for all that, I just walk away."

"Yeah it's not worth it."

"So, where yo boyfriend at? I meant to say why don't you have a man and kids?"

"Because these dudes ain't my type."

"You like saying that don't you?"

'Because it's true. They don't know how to treat women. All they want is sex, they act too immature, all they wanna do is get high or drunk and party and most of all they ain't got GOD in they life. That's a big no, no ... the number one rule for me.

It's a good thing you brought it up so we get it out the way. I don't have kids because I don't have sex, and I won't until I get married. So even if I do meet a guy that's my type he usually doesn't stay long after he finds out that he isn't getting none. So now you know too.'

She looked at him to see his reaction and she asked, "What do you think about that?"

JB took a deep breath and told her, "Umm, I guess if that's how you live that's how you live. I respect that, I mean it ain't like we in a relationship anyway, we only going to dinner. Hopefully I'll get lucky enough to just be your friend. I ain't trying to have sex with you."

Erica smiled. "I told you, you are a smooth talker, but there's something about you that you're holding inside. I'll find out what it is eventually."

They pulled up to the restaurant.

"Have you ever ate here before?"

"No, I never been to any of the restaurants out here."

"Well I done ate on the beach before, but not here. So this is a first for both of us."

Erica said, "I hope they have tables, I don't feel like waiting 30 minutes to eat."

"Me either that's why I made reservations for us." He got out of the car, walked around and opened the door.

Erica asked him, "Do you do this all the time?"

"Do what?"

"Open doors, are you really sweet or are you just doing it for me?"

"Tell you the truth, I never open the door for nobody before this so yeah, it's all for you."

"Well now I feel special."

They went inside and the host greeted them and showed them to their table.

"So Miss Erica, what are you looking for in a dude?

"A man not a boy. A God-fearing man, a working man. Someone that's mature, honest, respectable, faithful, responsible, strong and strong minded. Not to mention he has to look good, so far you got that one. Someone who is a gentleman, so far you have that one too. I like a man that can listen, you seem to have that."

"Well, so far I'm doing good, you gave me three out of the hundred."

Erica laughed. "Someone who is funny, I see that you have a little of that. Mainly like I said, a real man not a boy. So now to me what type of man are you? Please be honest because liars are not my type."

"I ain't gone to lie to you. I'm not your type. I mean I am a man, I'm not lil boy. I'm respectable, strong and strong-minded, but I don't think I'm your type. I knew that yesterday but I had to say whatever it took to get you to say yes.

I don't have a relationship with God, I mean I pray and stuff but I ain't been to church since I was a little boy, like 10 or 11."

JB paused...

The waitress came to the table. "Hello my name is Stacy and I'll be serving you tonight, what can I get you guys to drink? By the way you both look fabulous. I'm guessing anniversary or something?"

"No really this is our first date."

"Wow! Unbelievable, well I must say that dress and those heels are killer honey."

JB smiled and said, "I know right, that's what I said."

Erica smiled, "Thank you so much. I'll just have a water with lemon."

"And for you sir, what will it be?"

"I think I'll just have the same."

The server brought the drinks and some bread. The two ordered a light appetizer and continued their conversation.

Erica turned to JB and smiled, "Okay so where were we?"

"I was just telling you how I'm not your type but I want to be. I think you are somebody who can show me something different."

"Oh really?"

"Yeah I mean, and please don't get mad, and walk out screaming saying I'm leaving I'm calling a cab."

"You've had that happen to you?"

"No I'm just saying."

Erica replied, "I'm listening."

"Okay. First off I don't work, that car out there came from drug money."

Erica's eyes got big.

JB continued. "Hey I'm trying to be honest with you. I pray, but I don't really know about God. I smoke weed and I drink and I party a lot. I might do all that but I'm not a bad person, I ain't no goody two shoes either. I'm tired of that life though, all it does is bring trouble. It feels like I'm stuck and I can't get out, like the devil got chains on me. I can't get free to save my life.

I want to settle down one day, have some babies. You know have a wife and live straight but where I'm from that kind of life just don't happen for dudes like me. Not unless we get lucky and find a chic like you, but most of the broads around my way ain't nothing... I wanted to say something else. They don't want nothing but money. They want to fight, hang out and get high too. Women like you don't even look in my direction. Just like you said once, dudes find out they ain't getting none and they be gone. It's the same with me, once they find out who I really am, they be gone too."

Erica replied, "But see the thing is I obey God, as the Word says. I can't change and I refuse to change for anybody. You on the other team, you're living for yourself. You can change any time you get ready. If a guy doesn't want to be with me because I won't change, it's his loss not mine. If a girl doesn't want to be with you because you won't change then whose loss is it? Yours."

JB nodded his head. "You got a point there sister, that's why I like you. Dang! Did I just say that?"

They both laughed.

Erica replied, "Guess what though?"

"What?"

"I knew from the moment I saw you walk in my store that you wasn't my type, but there's something about you that catches my attention."

"Oh yeah?"

"Yeah and that's not easy to do. I guess when you are trained to think a certain way you become used to it. It's hard to see something else."

"So what do you see in me that catches your attention?"

'Hmmm let me see. I like your smile, and the way you carry yourself. I like how you talk, and I like how focused you are. I like the way you're looking into my eyes right now. It's almost scary, like a lion stalking its prey, but at the same time it's relaxing. Like, it makes me feel safe when I'm with you. I usually feel awkward, and uncomfortable. It's usually not too much to talk about but look at us, we haven't stopped yapping since Starbucks."

"I know right," JB responded.

"So what do you see in me Mr. Jonathan Griffin?"

JB had a strange look on his face. "How do you know my name?"

"Oh I saw it on a piece of paper in your glove box. I don't play. I took a quick picture of your vehicle registration before you got in the car."

"What!"

"Calm down, you never know who you're with these days. My mom is a detective, she taught me a lot. Say for instance you tell me your name is Tim and something happens. All I can tell the police is that your name was Tim. The name, age everything about you could be a lie. But not if I got the real info, don't worry about it I already deleted it."

"Scared of me? You the one that's scary. But that's some smart stuff."

"So Jonathan, tell me what you see."

"I see someone so pretty and so smart. Dang I mean you could be a counselor or something. I see a woman not a girl. Even though you're young, you got a good head on your shoulders. You know what else I see?"

"What?"

"I see you as somebody who could teach me a thing or two."

"Oh really?"

"Yeah and I see one more thing. It's kind of blurry and foggy but, it looks like I see my future wife sitting across from me."

Erica dropped her bread and threw up her hands. "That's it I can't take no more." She laughed. "This smooth talking is getting to me. I don't know what it is, I want to take you serious then I want to say you're full of it. I just can't put my finger on it."

"Why can't you just believe me? You think that I won't wanna be with you because you don't wanna have sex? I did fifteen months in prison. If I can do that I can be with you. It won't take me fifteen months to marry you."

"Excuse me! Hmmm you're pretty confident huh?"

"Well you like looking into my eyes, tell me if I'm lying."

Right then Erica felt something she had never felt before, and at that very moment she fell in love. She just wasn't going to tell JB that.

"What's the matter cat got your tongue?"

"No ... no but ummm, I honestly think we're moving way too fast, I mean this was just supposed to be dinner."

JB cut her off. "You right ... you right my bad, you ready to order?"

Erica whispered, "Yes."

Then out of nowhere Mr. Awkward Silent Moment himself shows his face ... 1, 2, 3, 4, 5, 6, 7, 8, almost 10 seconds passed before JB said anything, "Excuse me a minute, I'll be back. I am going to the bathroom." He started beating himself up, "Dang I was doing good."

He looked up at the ceiling and whispered, "*Yeah God... I think this might be the one.*" He paced back-and-forth in the bathroom wondering what he could say to get the conversation back running smoothly.

Then he hears an announcement come over the intercom. *Ladies and gentlemen I hope everyone is enjoying their meals tonight. I see we have a lot of fine looking couples in the building. Can I have the lights dimmed for a little bit? Okay everyone, if you thought you were having a good time think again, the night is about to get special. Let me introduce you to one of the baddest jazz bands in the land ... Soulful Symphony.*

JB figure if the two of them just listened to the band for the rest of the night he wouldn't have to talk as much. "*Okay God there you go, I owe you one.*"

JB left the restroom and went back to the table.

Erica a bit puzzled asked, "So is everything okay?"

"Yeah I'm straight, how are you? You alright?"

"I'm fine, this is really nice. I didn't know they were going to have a live band did you?"

"Yeah I knew."

It was clear that JB wasn't as verbal as he was before the restroom break so she asked him, "I didn't mess up the vibe did I? I hope I didn't make you uncomfortable."

"Naw, I'm good. It was my fault really."

Erica held up her phone. "See look, I deleted the picture. You passed my psycho tests. I think you're a cool guy." She got up and went to his side of the table. "Scoot over Mr. You don't mind if I sit next to you, do you?"

"Oh no not at all." He got a whiff of her perfume as she sat down. "Oh my God you smell so good."

She grabbed his hand. "I like music like this, it puts you in a mellow mood."

JB captivated by her presence said, "Yeah it does. No words just the instruments playing."

Erica asked him, "Do you dance?"

"Oh no, I don't do none of that."

"Why not, let me guess, it's not manly enough for you?"

That's when JB remembered that he forgot something. He waved at the waiter to come over.

"Naw see it ain't like that, it's just like I told you, where I'm from dudes like me don't do these kinds of things."

"Oh yeah, but we are not where you are from. We are on the beach at a very nice restaurant. This is a very nice band playing and you're with a very nice girl, wouldn't you agree?"

"Yes I would, that's why I decided that you deserve these."

Right when he said that the waiter walked behind Erica with a huge bouquet of white roses. Erica could not believe it, she blushed, smiled and almost came close to crying.

"You had all this planned?"

"Yep. I told you just one date and I would change how you see me."

"Yes you said that."

"Just think if you would have turned me down yesterday, we both would've missed out on each other."

"Yep. No one has ever did what you're doing tonight. I mean no one ever."

"And I never did it, no one ever deserved it, until now." He whispered in her ear, "*and now we can dance baby.*"

Erica's smile was so big. "I knew I put on this dress for a reason."

Erica felt so special, she felt like a princess in a fairytale. JB felt like the man, usually when he took a girl somewhere he never spent over $30 of $40 and it always ended in sex. That night when he added up the haircut, outfit, shoes, flowers and the dinner he spent well over $300 and there was no sex coming.

For the first time in his life he didn't seem to care much either.

They danced and talked for a while until about 10:45 pm.

Erica said, "I really hate to end the night early when it's going so good but it is getting late and I have to work in the morning."

JB said, "Yeah and I guess I better go look for work. If we are going to be together I can't sell drugs no more."

Erica said, "You are something else." "Erica, I do want you to know I want you."

Leaving the restaurant and walking to the car JB asked, "Can I have your number now? Now am I worthy enough to call you?"

Erica replied, "Yes you can have it. Only if I can have yours."

"No problem, so what kind of things do you like to do when you're not working beautiful?"

"Well I like to work out."

"I can tell, that body is right."

"Thank you. I also go to school so I'm a busy woman."

"Oh yeah, are you going to be a detective like your mother?

"No I am studying to be a lawyer. Maybe even a judge one day."

JB said, "That's what's up, I like that."

Erica continued, "I also go to church every Sunday and Wednesday."

"So, I ain't never going to see you then."

"You will don't worry, as a matter of fact since you picked the first date I get to pick the second one."

"Cool you name it."

"Anywhere?"

"Yep, anywhere, just tell me where you want to go."

"It is not where I wanna go is where I'm going ... to church if you want to get those chains broken, that's the way I know how. God can turn any situation around no matter how deep you're in."

JB thought about it. "Yeah I still do need to do something because the game crazy."

They pulled into the Starbucks parking lot. Erica pointed, "That's my car over there. I really had a good time tonight, thank you for everything."

"Oh it's nothing, you're very welcome. Really I gotta thank you."

"For what?"

JB responded, "For giving me a chance. Maybe God brought us together. If my Momma didn't love coffee, I would've never bought the gift card and I would've never met you."

"Yeah I wasn't even supposed to work Mother's Day. Melissa called off because she went to visit her mom in Alabama. So yeah the Lord works in mysterious ways. Alright I got to go but I'll call you tomorrow, probably on my break."

"Okay hit me. I'll walk you to your car. It's late plus don't forget ... I'm the new security guard."

Erica laughed.

"Hey you said it. Before you leave can I have a ...," JB paused because he was afraid to ask.

"I guess so, but don't grab my butt."

"Now do I look like someone who would do that?"

"Honestly yes you do, but never judge a book by its cover right? Even though you look like you would, I don't think you would do that to me."

"Yeah you different, good night."

Erica said, "Good night."

The night was over and JB had such a good time he forgot all about the shootout that went down earlier. However, reality doesn't take long to set in at all. It all came back to him. He still didn't wanna go home, and he still didn't put the battery back in his phone. He thought it might be best that he just wait till morning.

All he wanted to do was relax and go to sleep. He went and checked into a hotel and called it a night.

# CHAPTER 4

———— ⟨◇⟩ ————

The next morning JB was awakened out of his sleep by a knock on the door. He jumped up out of bed and started to panic. "Oh crap, oh crap, oh crap."

Everyone knows that most hotel rooms only have one door so there was nowhere he could run, but wait... there was a window. He ran to the window but there was no police anywhere in sight. He started talking to himself, *Oh Naw, see they think they slick. They hiding around the corner, damn, damn, damn.*

Just as he said that there was another knock on the door followed by a female's voice, "Housekeeping... housekeeping."

JB ran to the door and looked through the peephole and saw a short woman standing there with a card. He said to himself, *what the hell! If it's the police they got me, if I don't open the door they'll kick it down and come in and they still got me.*

He took a deep breath and he opened the door.

"Hello housekeeping, check out time, are you staying or leaving?"

JB looked down the hallway to the left, then he looked to the right, then he said, "I'm leaving" and took off. He dropped the room key on the cart and ran all the way to his car. Even though there was no sign of police, his heart was beating as if he was surrounded at gunpoint.

He couldn't take it no more he had to know what was going on back in the hood.

He put the battery back in his phone and saw that he had 35 missed calls and 152 Text messages. That wasn't surprising though, what was surprising is that the last hit came from Erica at 10 AM.

It read: *"Good morning you, I called you but it went straight to voicemail. I'm on my break. I just wanted to thank you again for a wonderful night last night, I had such a good time. You've been on my mind all morning. I'll call you when I get off at 2 o'clock. Have a nice day."*

JB had missed calls from his mom, Chris, Mike, Bruce, Jazz, Sam, Alvin and a few of his regular customers. There were a couple numbers in there that he didn't recognize, numbers that looked like law enforcement numbers, numbers he wasn't going to call back.

The first person he called was his best friend Mike.

Mike answered quickly, "Bro what's up boy? Everybody and they mama been trying to get in touch with you."

"I know but I wasn't trying to talk to nobody. I had to get my head clear right quick and figure out my next move."

"Boy troll been riding through the hood heavy."

"I know that's why I got missing, I ain't stupid. I ain't wit this paranoid crap, fool I can't even think straight. I feel like I've done killed somebody. What everybody talking 'bout?"

"Well, nobody ain't seen or heard nothing from Hippo or Rhino. You know he killed dude right?"

"Yeah I heard ... that's crazy Bro." Mike said,

"Yeah and them niggas going round telling everybody they looking for us."

JB responded, "Man I ain't worrying about them niggas, I wish I would see one of them."

Mike replied, "Bruce called me too, he straight."

"Cool, that's what's up, glad he good."

"He talking 'bout troll came up there asking 101 questions but they couldn't take him to jail because he ain't do nothing. They was trying to get him to snitch on you, Alvin and Hippo, but he said he ain't saying nothing."

JB asked, "So what's up with you?"

"I'm straight, they ain't even sweatin' me I don't think. All I did was fight, what's the most they can do? Hell I went home, they ain't even been by. They rolled by but they ain't stop. If they do get me for something I will just bond out. That's what you should do. Ain't no point in keep running, that's gone make it worse. Long as you keep running you ain't gone be able to go home.

Matter of fact where you stay last night?"

"Man I went to the Holiday Inn."

"So what you gone do, get a room every night? You know how much money you gonna spend doing that? Then eventually they gone get you anyway. The best thing you can do is turn yourself in and bond out right quick, and get a lawyer. Hell you'll be out in three to four hours. Then you can come back to the block. Boy it is a ghost town since that mess happened. It's just been me and Chris chilling.

I ain't heard from Alvin, but Sam did call me I forgot to say. He straight too, the police ain't sweating him either but he say he got a headache out of this world, he just taking it easy. I ain't heard from Chaz though."

JB said, "I had a missed call from Chaz, I just ain't text him back yet. Oh guess where I went last night?"

"Where?

"No no ... better yet guess WHO I was with."

"Oh boy who? Not Tiffany I hope."

JB annoyed said, "Hell no don't try me like that."

Joking, Mike said, "You know you crazy about Tiffany JB I don't even know why you acting."

"Naw, I used to be crazy about Tiffany, but for real I went and picked up Erica."

"Who? Who the hell is Erica?"

"Starbucks."

"Nooo! Swear to God! Nigga we knew you was in there trying to get the number, Chris said it."

"Yeah I had picked her up at 9 o'clock."

"You hit it?"

"Naw bro, she a virgin."

"A virgin! Punk, what the hell you posed to do with that?"

"That's how she was raised Bro, she a church girl. She cool though."

"She cool? Nigga what you gonna do with a church girl? You gonna mess around and get struck by lightning playing with God like that. What kind of lie you told to pull that one off?"

"I didn't lie bro, I told her everything about me."

"You ain't tell her you was just in a shoot-out."

JB laughed. "Naw, I ain't tell her that."

"I know you didn't."

"So where ya'll went?"

"We went to a jazz restaurant on the beach."

"Aww my dawg done went soft on me. Boy I ain't never known you to do no junk like that, and let me guess you paid for everything."

"Yeah I ain't gone lie I did."

Mike put the phone down and grabbed his head. He screamed, "Ya'll hear this world the pimp has lost his powers!" He picked the phone back up. "Dude you is officially not a player no more. You done broke the magic rule, nigga you didn't pay for the booty, you paid for the food not the booty. And you talking 'bout she cool, you sure it was Chaz that got hit with the bottle and not you? I guess next time you gone be trying to go to church?"

"Yep, matter of fact she said for our second date that's where we going."

"Oh she said... she said. You hear this world, this Nigga said *she* said. Boy check this out, I got a big fat blunt over here that you need to smoke. Like right now because you done went crazy. Damn I forgot you can't even come through. Man you really need to just go bond out right quick and get at me in a couple hours, this Nigga said he going to church with a virgin. I done heard it all."

"Bro you retarded, let me call my old girl. I just turned my phone back on and she done called like ten times."

"Man go bond out, get that junk over with."

"Yeah I hear you Mike, holla at you though."

"Okay bro be easy, bless."

JB replied "Yeah," and starts thinking about what Mike said. Maybe it was better to turn himself and instead of running some more. Mike was the one person he knew longer than anybody. The one he was closest to and the one he trusted. He was the one JB talked about everything with, but for the first time ever he felt that he and Mike did not see eye to eye.

Most always they agreed on everything; however, this time JB didn't agree with Mike concerning Erica and he didn't appreciate the comments Mike made about her. He felt the connection that he Erica shared the previous night and it was real. And he planned to keep seeing her regardless of what Mike said.

Yeah maybe Mike was right about turning himself in, but just not at that very moment. JB called his mom.

He let the phone ring a couple of times, as usual.

JB's mom answered, "Hello."

"Hey Ma."

"Boy where the hell you been? I've been calling you like crazy. I had to make sure you wasn't dead because I called the jail and they said you wasn't there."

"Well, I'm 'bout to be in there tonight because I'm trying to turn myself in."

"What! Hallelujah! Thank you Jesus my son done got smart."

"Well ma, you the one who told me to do it remember?"

"Yes I remember but when do you listen to me? That's good son, because the way police are killing boys today you don't want them to shoot you because they will."

"Naw, I'm turning myself in, bonding out and then getting a lawyer, but that's not all guess what else?"

"What's that?"

"I'm 'bout to go look for job."

"Oh Lord, thank you Father, this just keeps getting better and better. It must gone rain today, the good Lord doing all kinds of miracles signs and wonders. And where did all this positive energy come from all of a sudden?"

"Well I just had a long time to think. I mean I'm already 32, I ain't got no kids, no lady, nothing. I got a house and two cars but all I do is chill on the block all day every day and that junk starting to get boring."

JB's mom corrected him and said, "It should have been boring but that's good. I mean it sound good but you just gotta do it. Lord knows I want some grandbabies. Your sister will be down here in October, she got her a new boyfriend talking about they're trying to have a baby too."

"Oh yeah, that's what's up. Speaking of new relationships, remember I told you about the chic from Starbucks? We went out to eat last night on the beach. It was nice, we was dancing and everything, to jazz music."

"So you did go on the date, that's good Jonathan. Now I see where all this new 'I want to change my life' talk is coming from. I know it had to be a catch somewhere in there. I told you though Jonathan, don't go and mess this lil girl life up.

How old is she anyway?"

"She 26 and she in school to be a lawyer. She got no kids or nothing, she's straight and she feeling me."

"Feeling you, ha, ha. She don't know you that's why she feeling you."

"Naw ma, I told her about me, she know. We going to church too."

"Boy! Come over here and let me feel your head, make sure you ain't sick. You going to church so she must really be special. You go boy, make me proud. Make me think that I taught you something in life."

"You did Ma, and I thank you for never giving up on me, I love you."

Cynthia starts to cry. "I love you too son. I knew the whole time that you had a lot of potential; you just chose to use it for all the wrong things. You managed to get a house and two cars, very nice cars from selling drugs. If you just put all that same effort into the right thing you will be unstoppable, I see it in you."

"Yeah, I'm done with all this stupid stuff."

"The streets?"

"Yeah that's what I was about to say. I'm done with the streets. I just got off the phone with Mike before I called you and I just wasn't feeling him today for some reason, and you know that's my dawg. I'm just ready for something different. Now I gotta see what these people gone try to do with me. I might have to do a little time, hopefully not much if this lawyer does his job right."

"It ain't about the lawyer baby it is about God, you got to give it all to Him. Baby you can't just go around shooting at people, but you did it and now you gotta face the consequences. But I promise whatever happens is gone be alright if you give it to God."

"Yeah, I think I'm ready for something different. I'm about to get ready to go call this lawyer, then go look for a job. I might need to come take a shower at your house."

"You better hurry up, you know we 'bout to leave to go to the airport."

"Oh snap ma, I forgot all about the Mexico trip."

"Yes I'm so excited and ready and your Auntie is on her way over here right now. I can't believe you did that for me son thank you."

"You're welcome Ma, ya'll go have fun you deserve it. Call me when you get over there and get settled in, tell me if it looks like it do on TV."

"Right son, you know they hype everything up on TV to make you want to go."

"Yep, they do."

"Ok Jonathan, I'm going to finish getting ready."

"Alright ma. See you in a minute."

J3 came up with a plan. He was going to turn himself in, he didn't want Erica to find out that he was in jail so he had to make sure he talked to her first. He was going to have to wait till she went to school. That way maybe she would be busy for at least four hours that would give him time to get back out. He called a lawyer and set an appointment to go into the office.

He always kept clothes at his mother's house just in case of an emergency, so he went over there and took a shower. She didn't mention anything about the police when they spoke on the phone so he felt safe enough to take a chance. Even though he felt safe you never know with the police, they could be watching so he parked the car on the next street and snuck in through the back. He took the quickest shower he had ever taken, got dressed and was back out the door in less than ten minutes.

Little did he know things were about to take a turn for the worst.

He got a call from Mike, "Wassup bro?"

Mike talking fast said, "Boy you on the news."

"What!" "I swear to God it's on right now police are looking for five suspects involved in a shooting at a local convenience store yesterday morning. One victim died later at the hospital and a second, Terry Matthews, was badly wounded but injuries are not life-threatening."

JB cursed, "Damn."

Mike continued, "Oh... police are looking for a Gregory Behring, age 21, they say he is responsible for the murder of 28-year-old Williams. Four more shooters were spotted later on in the video as this horrific event continued. Police also say Chazerio Green, Alvin Green, Jonathan Griffin and Creg Barrington twin brother of Greg Barrington are being charged with felony possession of a firearm and public endangerment.

These individuals are still on the loose and are considered to be armed and dangerous. If you have any information or happen to know the whereabouts of these gentlemen you are asked to call Crime Stoppers at 1-800- crime stoppers. The number is on the bottom of the screen, callers can remain anonymous.

Bro, this is about to be crazy bro."

All JB could think about was what if Erica just saw what Mike just saw, it would be over just like that, but luckily she was at work. His thoughts went into a panic and he started questioning if there were TV's in Starbucks, Newspapers, etc. But what if she goes on break? He was going crazy.

He was lost in his thoughts until he heard Mike calling his name.

"JB... JB... you still there?"

"Oh yeah man, sorry... I blacked out for a minute, damn dawg on the news."

Mike replied, "Yeah and they go be playing that all day over and over. You better call your girl at Starbucks and make sure she doesn't see this."

"Yeah I know that's what I was thinking about."

"Maybe if you hurry up and turn yourself in they'll take your name off of it."

"Man, man. Now I know somebody is going to call my momma and tell her. Watch she'll call me in 'bout 5 minutes."

"So what you gone do?"

"Oh I am on the way to the lawyer office now. Then I'm fenna get it over with because this is crazy. They act like I killed somebody. Hey I'll hit you back in a minute I got a do something."

Mike said okay and hung up the phone.

JB came up with another plan; it didn't seem like plan A was going to work so it was time for Plan B.

He sent a text to Erica saying, "*Hey sweetie wassup? Sorry I missed your call, I was super tired. I'm glad you had a good time last night. I had a good time too. You make me want to try something different, get my life right. I can't wait to see you again. I would come up to your job to see you but I don't want to bug you like that, gotta give you some space. Anyways I gotta take my mom to the airport so she can go to Mexico. I'll call you when I'm done. You have a good day too.*"

He prayed that his little plan would buy him some time. He went to the lawyer's office just like everyone else and the lawyer suggested. They discussed what took place at the store, they talked about how much it would cost to represent JB and the most important thing they talked about was how much time he would probably have to spend locked up.

The lawyer told him that with his record he was looking at an easy 25 years. But for $15,000 he could get him maybe three years and some probation. Maybe less depending on the facts of the case which was too early to know being that it had only been 27 hours.

JB really didn't have a choice.

He had a pretty good business going selling weed and cocaine so over the years he probably made well over $200,000, but he also spent well over $200,000. Two cars with the rims, music systems and TVs, a house, expensive jewelry, a closet full of top name brand shoes and clothes and that wasn't it.

He and his boys probably smoked more weed than the nickel and dime hustler sold. His party life in the clubs wasn't cheap and the women he was attracted to didn't come cheap either. And with the new trip to Mexico he had just bought for his mom, the date and hotel he spent money on the night before, and this $2500 bond he was about to pay, his pockets were looking lower than they had looked in a while.

He just didn't have $15,000 sitting around like that. He only had about $3000 in the bank. He would have to do what he didn't want to do. He would have to make some plays. But how could he do that when all his product was at his house, and the police was watching that place like a hawk.

He didn't worry about it right then.

He told the lawyer that he would get back with him tomorrow and that he was going to bond out. Maybe that would give him enough time to obtain the down payment. He knew he could probably borrow money from Chris and Mike but he was their suppliers so chances are they wasn't gonna have that kind of cash lying around either. He went to the liquor store, grabbed a pint of Gin and poured a drink. He went to the bank and made the withdrawal and headed for the jailhouse.

So much was running through his mind. Twenty-five years, three years, $15,000, Erica. Or worse, what if the guys he shot at came back and tried to kill him.

Yes it was definitely time for something different.

JB was ready for a new life.

\* \* \*

He went to jail, bonded out and was back on the streets within two and half hours. He felt refreshed like the weight had been lifted off of his shoulders.

Well some of the weight.

He wasn't clear yet, he still didn't know if Erica had seen the news or not. He checked his phone and sure enough he had a text from Erica. He was scared to read it, but he did anyways, *"I got your text and was going to call you when I got off. I have school tonight so I'll call you on my first break at 5 o'clock hopefully you'll be done at the airport by then because I need to ask you something."*

He started to bang his head against the window of the car. The suspense was killing him. Did she know or did she not know? He couldn't take it; he wanted to text back and just ask her if she had seen the news, but if not he figured that might just make her want to watch it.

Then he thought about telling her the truth and that was the worst that could happen right now.

She could say I no longer want to talk to you. He didn't want that but, he had only known her for a day, it wasn't like he had feelings for her yet. That was just it, he did have some feelings, if not he wouldn't care if she found out or not.  He was rationalizing.

Once he went to jail to serve his sentence she would find out anyway. But hell by then, he thought, they would be deep into the relationship and she would love him enough to wait.

He didn't know what else to do. It was really messing with his mind. Erica was special, a rare catch. He thought about what his mom told him earlier, give it to God, so that's what he did now that he knew the police was no longer looking for him he felt safe to move as he wanted.

Most importantly he wasn't paranoid to step foot inside of his own house anymore.

He gave Mike a call.

The phone rang a few times and finally Mike picked up.

Mike answered giving JB a hard time, "Bro you ain't turn yourself in yet, what you waiting for?"

"Fool, I done went to jail and came back already what you talking 'bout?"

"Damn that was fast as hell, Nigga you ain't turn yourself in that quick."

"I swear, it only took 2 ½ hours. That's because I didn't go through a Bondsman. I had the money on me, I did a self-bond, its way faster."

'Oh that's what's up then, where you at? Come slide through."

"That's what I'm about to do, I just had to see what you was doing 'cause we need to talk."

"Oh man, I'm just chilling, Chris about to come over right quick too."

JB insisted, "Naw ya'll meet me at my house in 20 minutes, I got something for ya'll."

"Damn yesterday was Mother's Day, what today is home boy day? You giving out presents and shit?"

"Something like that, don't worry you gone like it."

"Okay bet ... that's what's up, I'm fenna tell Chris."

JB reminded him, "Yep, 20 minutes."

"Yeah."

JB sent Erica another text message. *"Hey guess what? I finished at the airport early. Give me a call when you get a chance, I can't stop thinking about you, I wanna hear your voice.*

He had to make it sound sweet because he was still hoping she didn't find out about the shooting.

He called Mike back, "Hello."

"Yeah Mike, I just thought about something. Ya'll can't come together."

"Why man, wassup?"

"Just trust me. You come to the front door and tell Chris to go around the block and come through the back."

"Huh?"

JB said, "Bro, trust me just do it."

"Alright."

When JB made it home he didn't see any cop cars or any suspicious looking vehicles parked on the street. He went inside.

It had only been a day but he was missing home like he hadn't been there in weeks. He went straight for the bathroom. He didn't even close the door, just dropped his pants down to his ankles flopped down on the toilet and started singing to himself.

He thought, *"Ain't nothing like a little relaxation."*

A couple minutes passed by and Mike pulled up in the drive way. He got out and rang the doorbell.

There was no answer so he rang it again.

He started talking to himself, *"Now I see the car so I know he in there."* He rang the doorbell again.

JB open the door wildly. "Nigga stop ringing my doorbell like you crazy."

"What the hell you doing in there boy?"

JB laughing said, "I was in the bathroom, can I go in peace?"

Mike clowning him said, "Yeah I can definitely tell you was in the john."

Laughing, they walk back inside. "So what's good man? What you got for me?"

"Just hold up, I'm fenna tell you, let's wait on Chris. Matter of fact where that nigga at?"

"I don't know I just saw him at the stop sign and I came around the block."

Ten long minutes passed before there was a knock on the back door.

JB opened the door. "Dang Chris, you forgot where I stayed at or something?"

"No you know I had to go to the store and get some blunts to smoke.

JB was just a little fearful and still on high alert. "You ain't seen no police did you?"

Chris getting smart with him said, "Now ask yourself that question again. If I would've seen the police, you wouldn't see me, make sense? I thought so."

"All right smart man, roll up then."

Mike looking for some liquor asked, "Where the truth? I know you got a bottle of Hennessey in the kitchen."

"Yeah it's in there, ain't no coke though."

"Aww man I'm so hurt? Well guess that means we got to drink it straight then. So what's up with this mafia meeting you calling Sir? What we fenna sit at the roundtable or something?"

JB laughing at them said, "Yep something like that."

Chris clowning JB said, "Okay King Arthur."

"Alright fools, hold on I'll be right back."

JB went into the garage and brought out two duffle bags. In one duffle bag there was 16 1/2 lbs. of weed, and 18 oz. of powder cocaine in the other, that's a half kilo. He brought the bags into the living room and dropped them on the table.

I need ya'll help on something. I gotta move this, I need the money for a lawyer. They talking about with my record I can get up to twenty-five years.

Chris said, "Twenty-five years, boy there ain't no way I could do twenty-five years Craig."

Mike chimed in, "Hell Naw. I'd go crazy too."

JB that's why I am paying the lawyer $15,000.

Chris said, "Damn."

"Mike replied, "JB man that ain't nothing for you, you got it big Baller."

"Man no I don't that's why I got to sell all this."

Mike asked, "What's in there? That one smell like weed so I know what's in that one."

JB unzipped the bags and dumped everything out on the table.

Chris's eyes got big ..."Damn that's a lot of stuff. He started counting... *one, two, three, and four*." JB said, "It's over 16 ½ lbs. and 18 oz."

Mike responded, "Yeah that is a lot."

Neither Mike nor Chris had ever seen that many drugs at one time.

Mike in disbelief said, "Damn dawg I knew you had it but I ain't know you had it like that. I thought I was supposed to be your best friend, and you holding out on me like this?"

Chris chimed in and said, "Yeah he holding out on both of us."

"Ya'll tripping ... that's why I called you over here. Ya'll can have all this man, I'm done."

Mike looked confused, "You what? What? You done?"

"Man I'm done selling drugs. I'm fenna let ya'll take over the business."

Mike still in shock said, "You serious or you joking bro?"

"I'm dead serious Mike I ain't playing, I'm tired."

Chris started rubbing his hands together, "Boy you crazy but I like your crazy. You fenna let us have all this? Everything?"

"Yeah but first you got help me sell it."

"Okay, Mr. Smart criminal, tell me how we gone have it all if we sell it all? I ain't the smartest man in the world but I know 2+2 don't equal what the hell you talking 'bout."

'He got a point JB. For once I'm on his side."

"Bro when I say I'm done I mean I'm done. And when I say you can have it all I ain't just talking 'bout what's on this table. I'm talking 'bout the plug, the customers, everybody and everything. I'm going to turn the whole thing over to you two. Once I'm finished paying this lawyer I'm getting a job and that's it.

It's enough right here on this table to make $30,000 easy. That's if you don't touch it. Just sell it like it is and if you break it down, cook the powder into crack then you talking 'bout the double that.

Between $60 and $80 grand.

All I need to make is $20,000 ... $15,000 for the lawyer and $5000 for myself. Ya'll can have the rest and build up from there. Between the two of ya'll, in a year if you do it right and be smart, then ya'll can be the new Kings of the city. You can supply the whole hood."

Chris smiling from ear to ear said, "Oh yeah, that's what I'm talking 'bout, but why are we doing this again? Why all of a sudden you wanna stop?"

"Because it's time for something new bro, I gotta live a new life."

"Chris I'll tell you what it is. He ain't gone tell you but I will. This joker done got with the chic from Starbucks and they fenna start going to church together."

"What!"

"Yeah Chris man, he told me this morning, ain't that something?"

"Say it ain't so, damn I wanted her. I ain't gone lie she was fine as hell. But she wasn't that fine enough to make me give all my drugs away. Hell I won't give a hooker half a joint. I damn show ain't fenna boy! I know you only got one head but if you had to two you would've just bumped both of them.

Boy that sex must have been the best sex in America, in the world and out of the world. That was some space sex, cybersex."

Mike cut in, "Chris."

"Yeah, what's up?"

"He ain't get none, she a virgin."

Chris had a puzzled dazed kind of look on his face. He looked up to the ceiling. Mike couldn't help but laugh at the way Chris was looking. Chris shook his head. "I have absolutely ran out of words. Yep, no words for that one. I'm getting drunk."

He poured a shot and swallowed it then poured another and swallowed that one too.

JB said, "I don't care what you say dawg. It's time bro, something different. I already got a house, two cars, I'm straight. I really don't need to sell drugs anyway. I've just been doing it for fun and drawing attention to myself."

Mike full of himself said, "Well I like attention, and I like money."

Again JB felt that disconnection with Mike.

Chris chimed in and said, "Me too, I like drugs and money too."

JB's phone rang, "Hello."

It was Erica. *"Hey there, you're a hard man to reach I see."* He could tell by the tone of her voice and how she started the conversation that she knew nothing about the shooting, at least not yet.

He jumped up and walked out of the room. "Oh no I just had a few things to handle this morning, how you doing?"

Mike clowning JB said, "See that's her right there, I bet that's Starbucks."

"I was just sitting here talking with the fellas about something. I'm fine though how are you?"

*"I'm fantastic actually. I'm at school on my break. I've been thinking about you all morning."*

JB smiling like a kid with candy said, "Oh yeah? Same here. I was just telling them that I'm going to be leaving the drug business and living legit."

*"Okay? And what did they have to say about it?"*

"Ummm, they just laughed like I was out of my mind. It's all good. It's crazy though because my whole life me and Mike been like brothers. Now I feel like we have a space between us."

*"Yeah it happens like that. Sometimes when you're going down a road and you come to a split, one wants to go one way and one wants to go the other way. Sad to say but when God calls you He only calls you, sometimes you lose your friends in the process. Everyone can't go where you go Johnathon."*

"You know you sound just like my momma, you sure you don't know her?

Erica giggled and said, *"Women know best."*

"You came in my life at just the right time Erica." "Oh yeah how is that?" "With all I got going on I need somebody like you close to me."

She giggled again, *"That's good because I like being close to you. But my short break is over I have to call you when I get out okay?"*

JB still grinning said, "Okay you do that."

*"Okay bye Jonathan."*

"Bye."

JB walked back into the living room.

Chris clowned him, "Okay lover boy, retired king pin, drug smuggler what we fenna do with all this stuff you ain't tell us you had?"

Mike chiming in said, "Yeah you see how he been laying low on us? We wondered how you've been buying these cars."

"Fool you got a car too."

"Yeah but I ain't got two cars and a house."

Chris said, "We will in a minute baby."

"You heard him Mike, you will in a minute. Now I gotta couple missed calls so I'm gonna hit them back and see if they still need something. Ya'll start getting on the phone with ya'll people. We gotta get this money. I need $5,000 to get the lawyer started. Then I'll pay him another $10,000 and then I keep the last $5,000. Then ya'll take the rest, deal?"

Mike and Chris together, "Deal."

JB strategizing said, "Now this the plan because I still don't know if the police watching or not. So Mike me and you gone leave like nothing happened, get in the car and go. Chris you gone take two pounds and two ounces out the back door. Take it to your house that way if we get pulled or something we don't go to jail. We'll meet back at your house then we'll go to the block from there. When we sell out we will come back to the house drop off the money and grab more.

Once we get the $20,000 then ya'll split the rest and take it to ya'll cribs. That's when I'll tell my connect that I'm handing everything over and he gone be dealing with ya'll from now on.

I'll tell all the customers the same thing. All ya'll gotta do is sell the stuff. Don't be trying to do all that extra crap. Just run the business smooth and ya'll won't have no problems. If everything go right we should have the $20,000 in about two days."

Chris couldn't believe what he was hearing, "Two days! Dang it move like that?"

"Yes, bro it moved just like that. Ya'll ready?"

Chris said, "Hold on let me get another shot."

"Mike what's wrong with him? I'm talking about ready to get this money."

"Oh yeah I'm ready boy." Mike smirking said, "I'm definitely ready."

Everything went as planned, the three of them moved the drugs quietly, smart and safe. They also moved it fast, so fast it was all gone that same night. JB had calculated the time wrong. He estimated it as if he was working alone, but with the three of them working together it took no time at all.

He paid the lawyer, kept $5000 for himself and gave the rest to Chris and Mike just as he promised.

He was satisfied and they were so happy that they decided to celebrate.

However, JB didn't want to celebrate, he had talked to Erica again when she got out of school and invited her over to watch some movies at his house.

He was finally out. He did what he said he wanted to do. And that was to try something different.

# CHAPTER 5

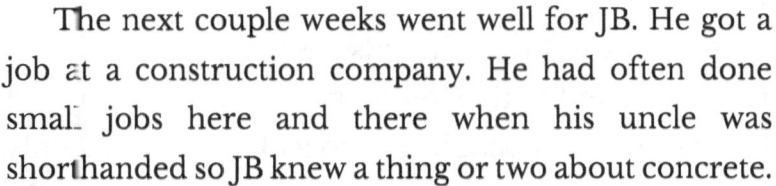

The next couple weeks went well for JB. He got a job at a construction company. He had often done small jobs here and there when his uncle was shorthanded so JB knew a thing or two about concrete.

The owner started JB at $15 an hour.

It was hard work but it was money. It was not like selling drugs where he could make $700 in ten minutes but at least he didn't have to look over his shoulder and that definitely was better than the fast money.

Mike and Chris stayed busy working their new business while he stayed busy with his new girlfriend.

He and Erica were getting closer and closer. He had even been to church a few times, and that's where he met you know who, Erica's mom. He was so nervous but when she said hello he was shocked.

She was nice to him.

He quickly found out that when you're a new face in church everyone wants to know who you are.

Every Sunday he went there was someone new introducing themselves and welcoming him to the church. They asked lots of questions like "What brings you to our church?" "Are you Erica's boyfriend?" "Are you saved?"

A couple of Erica's friends even said that JB looked very familiar, but they didn't know him. Everyone JB knew were street people, and to let him tell it the only people church people knew was other church people. Even if that were true no one said that church people don't watch the news.

JB was living so good for the past couple of weeks he totally forgot about the police.

Even though he had turned himself in and they were no longer looking for him there was still a search for the other four suspects.

Early one Sunday morning the TV showed an update: *Police are still searching for the suspects involved in a homicide that took place at the Marathon gas station in Petersburg. Three weeks ago one of the suspects Jonathan Griffin turned himself in and is out on bond, but the other four suspects Greg, Creg, Chazzelio & Alvin still remain on the loose.* He had no idea that his perfect world was soon going to crumble.

One day he and Erica got to the church and Shannon, one of Erica's friends pulled her to the side.

"Erica, remember I told you that I thought your friend looks familiar?"

"Yes girl, why do you know him?"

"No, I don't know him, how well do you know him?"

Erica replied, "I mean I didn't grow up with him and go to the same middle school but I know him a little bit why?"

"Erica, I saw him on the news this morning."

"Huh, what do you mean?"

"Listen, remember we heard about those people shooting at that one store?"

"Yeah so?"

"Erica... girl he was with them."

"What!"

"Yes girl."

"Shannon, are you sure you seen him?"

"Umm yeah ain't his name Jonathan something?"

"Yes. Oh my God, he told me he used to sell drugs but he ain't tell me he was shooting at people."

"I'm sorry I didn't know if you knew or not but I had to warn you just in case you didn't, you my girl."

"Yeah you my girl too, thank you."

"You welcome."

"But he's so nice and sweet, I never met nobody like him before."

"Hey you never know. Alright I don't want to keep you too long, go on and get back over there."

"Okay thank you again."

"You're welcome."

Erica didn't know what to think. She definitely wasn't going to make a scene in church so she just pretended like she didn't know. She couldn't hardly pay attention her mind was racing so much, she got down on her knees and prayed.

Once church was over and they got into the car that's when she popped the question. "Jonathan, did you enjoy today's service?"

"Yeah it was good, the pastor was speaking some real stuff."

"Ok, so I won't even beat around the bush, umm."

JB said, "What's up baby? Spit it out."

Erica paused for a second. That was the first time JB had ever called her baby. The 40% of anger she had in her now dropped to 20%, but she asked the question anyway. "Were you on the news for a shooting this morning?"

'What?"

'You heard me."

"Yes I did hear you but you just caught me off-guard. Yeah I was on the news, but that was for a something that happened before I knew you. And I know you mad."

"Yes, I'm mad that you lied to me and I told you I don't like liars, I introduced you to my mom, she's gonna kill me when she finds out."

JB thought about what she had just said. Erica's mom was a detective, how could she not have already known? "But baby listen."

"Stop calling me baby, why do you keep calling me baby?"

"That's what you are, I mean I thought that's what you were."

"Jonathan, we are not in a relationship we're just friends."

"I know but I'm ready to change that right now today, in this car. I knew you for almost a whole month now. We talk every day, you say you can't stop thinking about me and you know I can't stop thinking about you either. Look at me, I went to church three weeks in a row. That's more than I've been in over 15 years.

I don't want nobody but you Erica. I stopped selling drugs and got a job for you. I spend more time with you than with my best friend I knew since I was five years old. I want you, I told you that the first night remember?"

"Yes, but you shoot at people."

"Now you know I've changed. I'm not the same person no more baby. I'm sorry, no I take that back I'm not sorry. Can I call you baby? Tell me now."

Erica took a deep breath. Everything told her to say no but her heart made her say yes. "Yes baby, you can call me baby."

And that's when JB and Erica kissed for the first time

"But Jonathan, listen to me, I'm not going to do this if you can't promise me you're done. No, as a matter of fact you already promised me, now you have to show me."

"I'm showing you."

"Yeah Jonathan but is has only been 3 ½ weeks. I'm talking about two months, three months, or a year. You can't ever go back to the streets, or I won't be with you."

"Don't worry baby I'm not going back. But I have to tell you something though and I hope you don't get mad I was going to wait but since we're on the subject I gotta tell you."

"Oh no, what now?"

"I might have to go do some time. Even though it happened already I still ain't go to court yet."

"I can't believe this, that's why I took that picture. I had a feeling something was up with you. I was stupid though, I let your smooth talking trick me."

"I did not trick you Erica."

"Yes you did, I should've followed my first mind. I should've just let you walk out the store."

JB made a right on the next block and pulled over to the side of the rode. He put his head on the steering wheel. "So you gonna leave me? Huh?"

"How much time is some time, Jonathan?

"Are you gonna leave me? Tell me if you're going to leave me first."

"No tell me how much time first."

"It shouldn't matter Erica.

"Yeah right of course it matters. I've been taking you to church with me. My mother thinks you're a nice guy. I can't have a boyfriend in prison. Do you know how that will make me look? I have things going for myself, I'm in school."

She started to cry and at that very moment JB phone rings. It was his Auntie. "Hold on baby this my auntie calling me. Hey Auntie how you doing?"

*"I'm okay but your mom is not, you need to come to the hospital she done had a heart attack."*

"What!"

JB yelled so loud he made Erica jump.

He hung up the phone, put the car in drive and sped off.

"*What ... what happened?*"

"My momma just had a heart attack."

"Oh my GOD Lord Jesus. I gotta pray for her."

JB rushed all the way to the hospital.

"Baby please slow down you're scaring me. We don't need three people in the hospital. What happened? How did she have a heart attack? What caused it?"

"I don't know. She didn't say, I hung up."

"Yeah, I think you might have hung up too quick. You didn't even see what room number she was in. Here give me the phone I'll call her back."

Erica called JB's Aunt back.

Aunt Janice answered, "Hello, JB are you on your way?" She didn't expect to hear someone else's voice.

Erica responded, "Hello... yes ma'am we are on our way."

Aunt Janice was surprised and asked, "Who is this? May I ask who I'm speaking with?"

"Yes you may, this is Erica, JB's girlfriend."

JB looked over and saw Erica smiling at him. She had the cutest little face. She might have been mad about him being involved in the shooting and going to do time, but that priceless look on her face said something totally different. More like an *'I love you, I'm not going anywhere so if you asked me to marry you right now today I'd say yes kind of look.'*

At least that's how JB took it.

He had other things on his mind though it was just nice to hear her say that.

*"His girlfriend? When did he get one of those? I didn't know he had a girlfriend. Oh you must be the girl from Starbucks his mom told me he met."*

"Yep that's me Ms. Starbucks. Anyways how is his mom doing? And we need to know what room she's in, we'll be there in about five minutes, the way he's driving maybe two."

"So far it looks like she'll be fine. The doctors are running some tests. They say she may have over worked herself. Maybe all that excitement in Mexico a couple weeks ago might have caught up with her but I think she'll be fine. We're up here in 335."

"Okay we'll be there soon."

"Okay Erica, tell JB that his auntie said drive safely."

"Okay, bye."

"Bye, see you two soon."

"She said they still running tests but they think that too much excitement could have led up to it. Your aunt said she might have worked herself up too much in Mexico."

"Well she sho ain't gotta worry about me sending her on a trip no more."

"Oh you sent her to Mexico?"

"Yeah for a Mother's Day gift."

"Wow that was nice."

"Yeah never again. And she probably need to slow down on drinking all that coffee too. So I'm your boyfriend, huh?" He said in a joking way.

"I knew you was gone say that Jonathan."

"You the one said it. It's cool, I like future husband better though." He said that with a more serious tone.

"I bet you do. We'll talk about all this later; let's go check on your mom."

They arrived at the hospital and went to 335 on the third floor.

They walked in and saw Janice sitting by the bed. Erica spoke first, "Hello nice to meet you."

Aunt Janice responded, "Nice to meet you too, you're pretty."

"Thank you, so are you."

When JB saw his mom he became very sad. His facial expression and body language said it all. He looked like a three-year-old kid who just fell down and didn't know how to get up; he was crushed. His Aunt Janice and Erica comforted him and assured him that everything would be alright.

Two hours went by and Cynthia finally woke up.

JB rushed over to ask his mom how she felt. The doctors ordered everyone out so they could run another test.

Erica told JB that she had a few things to do and to call to give her an update. She had to study for an exam the teacher was giving the class first thing Monday morning. She told JB that he didn't have to leave she would call a cab or have a friend come pick her up. But Janice said, "No I'm about to leave also, where do you live? I can give you a ride it's no problem."

The two said their goodbyes and they left.

JB waited in the hallway thinking about everything. His mom, the shooting & going to prison for three years. He and Erica still hadn't talked about it. He thought to himself what if he was in prison and his mom had another heart attack, what would he do?

He thought about his own life on the streets and his new life working, going to church and how much fun he would be missing.

He liked Erica but was he really about the life of settling down or was he just kidding himself? Could he really stick to his word and keep his promise to her? Could he stay away from the streets forever and never go back, ever?

The nurse came out of the room and told him that his mom would most likely be staying at the hospital for at least a week. They found tumors growing in her stomach.

JB didn't know what to say.

The medical staff explained to JB what these tumors were and that if not taken care of immediately, they would turn into cancer. JB was devastated, he continued to talk to the doctors then he went back into the room and sat next to his mother.

He and his mom talked quietly for a while. That's when they heard a knock on the door.

JB answered, "Come in."

A tall dark man entered the room. JB's first thought was, *Could this strange man be his father?* "What's up man? Can I help you?"

Then JB took a closer look and realized that he was the pastor from the church.  He looked totally different without the big robe on. He had on regular clothes, jeans and a polo shirt.

Pastor Frank asked, "You don't recognize me in my street clothes do you?"

JB responded, "Oh yeah, I didn't at first but I know now, how you doing pastor?"

"How did you know we was here?"

"Erica called me about forty-five minutes ago and asked me if she could come and pray over her mother-in-law."

JB's eyebrows raised and he replied in disbelief, "Oh she did?"

JB knew right then that he had her, she had previously referred to him as boyfriend and now Cynthia was mother-in-law. He never asked her to do any of that. She took it upon herself to call his aunt in the car, and now she had just sent the pastor to the hospital to pray for his mother.

There was no way she was going anywhere; in his eyes she was wife material. His respect level for her grew higher. He also saw that the church wasn't so bad after all, he had felt the love when he was at church but now the church had brought the love to him.

Pastor Frank responded, "Yes she insisted that I come down and see about your mom."

JB's mom spoke up and said, "JB I like that girl, that's the best one I done seen you with. You make sure you keep her."

Pastor Frank chimed in, "Yes Erica is a nice young lady. I knew her grandfather and family when she was a baby, I watched her grow up."

"So you're not her grandpa?"

"Oh no he was senior pastor. Her grandfather founded the church. He passed away two years ago."

Cynthia replied, "Well I thank you sir for coming."

Pastor Frank said, "You're welcome but you don't have to thank me I'm just doing my job. I work for the good Lord, when he sends me on an assignment I don't ask no questions I just go. Now are you having pain anywhere?"

Cynthia replied, "In my chest and my stomach, but my whole body feels weak."

Pastor Frank asked her, "Well do you believe God to be a healer?"

"Yes I do Pastor."

"And do you know that there is nothing that he can't do? No matter what the tests say, no matter what the doctors say, God has the last word."

Cynthia responded, "Amen."

"Now, Ms. Cynthia, if you don't mind I'm going to put one hand on your chest and one hand on your stomach. I'm going to pray, and we're going to ask God to heal you right here today."

Cynthia closed her eyes and JB came over and held her hand.

Pastor Frank began praying: *Dear Father God, in Jesus mighty name I pray to you today. We ask that you lay your powerful hands on this woman right now Father GOD. Heal her of any sicknesses that may be trying to take over her body. We ask that you get rid of all the pain Father God. We know that there is no medicine like the power of the blood of Jesus. Hallelujah we praise your holy name.*

*Send a wave of healing Father GOD, cancel all negative reports Lord. The devil is a lie and we will not believe anything he says. Come right now LORD, step in and operate on this woman so that when the doctors come in they'll say ma'am you can go home our computers and tests were wrong.*

*We ask you for that today Lord. We pray for that and we have all faith that it will happen. We thank you Lord Father God because we believe that it has already happened. That's just how fast you work. We love you forever God, we receive you God, and we give you all of the glory.*

*In Jesus mighty name we pray and everyone say Amen*

They all talked for about ten more minutes. JB decided he would stay the rest of the night.

Erica called him at least once every hour to check up on Cynthia. Around 11 PM that night JB fell asleep in the chair next to the bed holding his mom's hand.

* * *

JB went to work in the morning and afterwards came home to shower. Erica went over after school and both she and JB went to the hospital to sit with Cynthia.

It wasn't long before the doctors had removed the tumors and Cynthia was able to return home.

A few more weeks went by and during that time JB's lawyer had begun working hard on the case. He told JB that the best thing he could probably do was get him down to two years followed by three years of probation, a suspended sentence of five years.

JB still wanted to see if he could fight for lesser time.

One day Erica sat JB down and said, "We need to talk."

"Wassup baby?"

"I know you thought I forgot but I didn't. I wanna know how much time you have to do."

"I don't know the lawyer is still going over the case."

"So he hasn't told you anything?"

JB didn't want to say three to twenty-five years so he lied.

"No he wants to wait, he doesn't want to get my hopes up. But I don't think it's going to be long because I've paid him $15,000."

Erica left it alone, but she felt something wasn't right.

JB still wasn't convinced that Erica would stick around if he was gone to prison. As long as they were face to face and just a phone call away, he knew he had her, but two years he wasn't so sure about. Now it was time for him to ask her a serious question.

"Hey baby..."

'Yes Jonathan?"

'I have been watching you ever since I met you. You are different from any girl I ever been with. I thanked you before but I wanna thank you again for everything. But that's not what I want to ask you. I want to know do you love me."

"Yes I do Jonathan."

JB got the answer he wanted to hear but still he seemed surprised to hear it. "You do?"

"Yes, honestly, you are way different from anybody I ever dated before too, but I think I loved you the first night we went to dinner on the beach."

JB shocked by Erica's words said, "Wow! So you're way good at keeping secrets huh?"

"Yeah I hold a lot in, I guess it is my defense mechanism."

They both laughed.

JB responded, "Yeah I also notice you keep asking me about this time, how much I'm getting. You say you love me but how much time would it take for you to leave me?"

"Ummm how am I supposed to answer that? I don't know, I mean I don't want to leave you at all, but I don't want to get my feelings involved then you leave me."

JB, reassuring Erica of how he felt said, "So how about we don't leave each other."

Erica looked confused. "Huh?"

JB replied, "I want you to move in with me, I'm tired of saying good night and hanging up the phone. Every day I see you with your hair done. I'm ready to see you when it is not done. I want to say good night and you still be right there."

"Oh my God are you sure, so fast?"

' It has been two whole months what are we waiting for? We both love each other."

Erica surprised said, "You love me?

"A little bit. Naw I'm just playing; heck yeah I love you girl and I want you to move in, please."

Erica just smiled and said okay.

JB laughing said, "I hope you can cook."

The next morning JB hired a moving company and Erica moved in. Ever since JB had left Chris and Mike alone in their drug world he and Mike had only spoken two or three times. He knew that he and Mike were growing apart.

Mike knew it too and he wasn't happy about it.

One day JB called Mike just to say hello. The phone rang and Mike answered, *"What's up Ghost man? I see you woke up from the dead."*

JB replied, "I been busy man, working and stuff. Gotta make sure my momma straight now that she out the hospital. What's been up with you though?"

Mike responded, *"Oh dude everything good over here. I got the block booming like crazy. Boy I'm making bout $1500 a night, easy."*

JB replied, "Yeah man that's what's up. I miss that fast money. This job working me to death and I ain't even making $1000 in a week. But its cool cause Erica working too so we straight."

"Yeah you still with her huh? No wonder you ain't got no time for yo boys no more."

JB responded, "It ain't like that though."

Mike blew him off, "Yeah right I never thought that a chic would come between us, not many as we done hit together tag team."

"Mike... keep Erica out of this bro, she ain't got nothing to do with it. It's my own choice to better my life."

"Yeah whatever man, you can *better* your life all you want, I know you better come to my birthday party Friday that's all I know."

"Damn Mike man, I forgot yo birthday was this week. You know I'm gone be there. Hey was up with that fool Chris?"

"Oh Chris straight too, he done bought him a car now."

"What!"

"Yeah but he gotta get it fixed because he already wrecked it being drunk. Man, that joker be high all the time. He ain't never sober. You know how he smokes a joint every fifteen minutes."

JB replied, "Yeah that fool crazy."

Mike said, "Naw that ain't nothing, now he's on that coke heavy. Everyday all day, I don't know how he even make money he put so much of it in his nose."

JB responded, "Boy he needs to calm that mess down, that's one thing you can't do is get high on your own supply."

Mike replied, "They still ain't found Hippo and rhino yet."

JB said, "I don't know how, they both weigh over 400 lbs. And they always be together so how you can't see 800 lbs. walking down the street."

Mike replied, "They caught Alvin and Chaz though. They both bonded out but I don't think they got no lawyer money."

JB boldly told Mike, "Why don't you help them out with the money, making $1,500 a night easy?"

Mike brushed him off, "Man..."

"Yeah you ain't got nothing to say 'bout that huh?"

"Hey you know what JB, I got moves to make I'll holla at you later player."

"Yeah I'll be over there Friday."

"Cool."

JB said, "Yep."

After JB hung up with Mike he called Chris. JB whispered to himself, "*Pick up this phone fool.*"

Chris finally answered, "Hello."

"What's up Chris man?"

"Wassup JB I ain't talked to you in a while."

"I know man I've been handling a lot of business lately. How you been though, you taking care of yourself?"

"Yeah why you ask that? I'm doing good. Boy I gotta tell you thank you, you put me on my feet."

JB could hear in Chris' voice that he was high. He was talking extra slow. Normally Chris couldn't get out a whole sentence without telling some kind of joke. This wasn't Chris on the phone, this was someone else. "Hey Chris man I heard you been snorting powder wassup with that?"

Chris feeling defensive said, "Man, who told you that? Yeah I do so what, you know me. I always handle my drugs."

"Chris weed ain't Coke and coke ain't weed."

"Yeah but what is coke and weed together? Boy I'm telling you I be higher than a monkey taking a dump on the moon. Now that's high."

Okay there was the joke JB was waiting for. JB had also known Chris his whole life so he saw Chris pretty messed up, numerous times.

Maybe Mike was over exaggerating just a little bit. He was known to do that from time to time. But JB wanted to be sure so he asked Chris again. "Man you sure you alright, you ain't letting it get the best of you are you?"

"Man ... JB let me tell you something. Mohammed Ali couldn't get the best of me if I was handcuffed to his boxing glove. Boy I'm a rider, a champion. I'm good baby, I still got girls and I'm still making money thanks to you. I ain't gone forget you boy. When I buy me a house next to the Playboy mansion I'm gone invite you and Starbucks over there so ya'll can have a little fun. Come on tell the truth she like girls too, don't she?"

"Okay, Chris you still a fool, boy you ain't gone never stop tripping. Don't matter if you high or sober." He told Chris he would talk to him later and the two hung up.

When Erica got home that night he had a surprise waiting for her. It was movie night so he ordered pizzas but she had no idea what kind of toppings would be on them. After she had taken a shower and got cleaned up it was time to eat.

JB put the movie in the DVD player and sat down.

"Baby, tonight I ordered you your own pizza."

Erica replied, "I wondered why it was two instead of one. You know I ain't going to eat a whole pizza."

"You don't have to, you can take some to work tomorrow for lunch. I just know you don't like mushrooms so I got you pepperoni and sausage."

"Well thank you, but why didn't you fix my plate while I was in the shower like you always do?"

"Oh, because I was on the phone with Momma."

"Oh okay," she replied.

Erica opened the pizza box to find a two-carat diamond gold engagement ring sitting on a napkin in the middle of the pizza. She was only 5'4" tall but she jumped so high her head almost hit the ceiling fan.

Tears forming in her eyes she screamed, "Oh my God, Oh my God, Oh my God."

JB aimed the remote at the TV and the DVD player began to play soft romantic music.

Erica couldn't keep the tears inside. They flowed like a rushing river of water after a dam had broken. JB got down on one knee and grabbed her hand and said, "Erica, a.k.a. Miss Starbucks... Ever since I met you I've been in another world. You came along and changed my life. I don't ever want to go a day without you, you make me so happy, and I didn't even know I could feel like this. I can't wait one minute longer. I have to know now, would you become Mrs. Erika Starbucks Griffin?

Will you marry me?"

Erica was speechless. She looked as if she was in the beginning stages of an asthma attack. She finally spoke, "We can leave out the Starbucks, I know nobody but Chris got you calling me that. But yes Jonathan Griffin I will marry you."

They hugged and kissed and they held each other.

"See I told you it wouldn't take that long for me to marry you."

She hit him on the arm. "Alright now Jonathan don't get cocky."

JB pinched her on the butt.

"Nope sir. This is only an engagement. You still have to wait until the honeymoon."

"Dang."

"Yes I can't believe it. This ring is humongous. It's so beautiful and shiny. Thank you so much I have to go call my mom now."

Everything was going well for JB. However, just when things are going good that's the devil's favorite time to step in, kill, steal and destroy.

Friday came and Erica was headed to work.

"Erica baby today is Mike's birthday so after work I'm coming home to take a shower then I'm going to hang out with him."

"Okay Jonathan... what is he going to be doing?"

'Ain't no telling but I promise I will be good."

"You better, don't forget our talk."

"I know baby but that's my best friend, he already calling me a ghost because he never sees me. I've known him my whole life and I ain't never missed his birthday."

"Ok I know that's your friend so go have fun, just don't have too much fun."

"Okay baby give me a kiss."

Erica left and one hour later JB left.

After work he did just what he said he would. He took a shower and went to the block. There was people everywhere. He hadn't seen that many people on the block since he threw a New Year's party two years before. When he saw Mike he was impressed to see how far he had come with the business.

Mike told him days before that he was now making $2500 a day but he didn't really believe him, not until then. Mike had on a bunch of nice jewelry. He looked like a young Mr. T or some big-time rapper getting ready for a video shoot. He had two big $300 bottles of champagne, one in each hand, and he was wearing Versace from head to toe - socks, boxers, earrings and even his deodorant was Versace.

JB greeted him with their usual hand shake.

"Wassup I see you doing your thing. Happy birthday boy."

"Thank you. I told you I was living didn't I?"

"Yeah you did."

"But you didn't believe me did you JB? Check this out I just bought this today fool."

Mike walked JB over to a car sitting on the side of the road. It was a 2014 Mercedes Benz. It was an $80,000 car.

"This yours boy?!"

"Mine dawg. I traded my car and gave the lot 20,000 in cash. The people at the lot ain't know what to do. They gave me the keys, man I'm making payments but I'll be finished in two months watch. Then I'm gonna buy a boat. That connect you gave me, he love me, I'm bringing him so much money it's a shame. You was right, this my city now."

Changing the subject JB asked, "Where Chris at?"

"Man that busta around here somewhere chasing after them raggedy girls. Here boy get some of this drink."

Mike didn't seem like he was too concerned with Chris and JB could sense that. Really it seemed like Mike wasn't too concerned about anyone but himself. "Naw I'm straight man, I ain't had nothing to drink in almost 2 months."

' Man that heffa done turned you all the way out."

"Hey chill out bruh, now you trippin. I told you to keep her out of this. That's my fiancée and she ain't did nothing, I chose to do this on my own."

'Your fiancée!"

JB cut him off. "Say it. I dare you to say it."

"Fool what you gone fight me over a lame chick? A church girl."

JB brushed him off and said, "Nigga you need to go to church. Man whatever I ain't fenna argue with you, where Chris?" JB walked away and went to find Chris. There were all kinds of women coming up to him saying things like, *"hey John-John where you been let's go get a room." "Hey JB you a church boy now you don't know us." "Hey JB you think you too good for the hood."*

Just then JB ran into Chaz. "Chaz what's up gangsta...? I heard they came and got you."

"Yeah but you see where I'm at don't you. They can't stop nothing, hey matter of fact I know where them Niggas at."

JB said, "Naw bro I ain't on that, and you shouldn't be either."

"Damn dawg you really did go Jesus freak on us."

"It ain't that, I'm just on some new stuff right now. I'm trying to stay out of jail, hell I just paid $15,000 so I can get two years. Don't you know they was trying to give me 25? You better get a lawyer talking about you know where they at. And they can stay where they at. After this party I'm taking my black butt home."

Chaz blew him off, "Nigga you trippin."

JB replied, "No you trippin, look at Hippo, he can't run forever. He fenna do life when they catch him, if they don't kill him because he stupid enough to shoot at them and try to get away, and you know that don't never work."

Bruce came walking up, he was walking with a limp. He reached out and hugged JB... "JB, JB, JB wassup baby?"

"Hey man ... yeah I see you walking now, how yo leg feeling?"

"Man it's getting better but I still gotta limp a little bit. I got a metal rod going right up here and like 15 screws."

JB responded, "Damn dawg my bad."

'It's cool, it is what it is."

JB still looking for Chris asked, "Hey ya'll seen Chris?"

Chaz said, "Yeah there go Chris right there."

Just like Mike, Chris was wearing jewelry too, just not nearly as much but you could tell he was getting money. JB walked over where he was sitting with the bunch of girls.

"Chris boy wassup?"

Chris looked up with white stuff all over his nose.

"Wassup JB? He jumped up and gave JB a big hug, and told the girls, "Hey ya'll this is the man that started all this right here. He is the one who put me and Mike on. Might as well say this kingpin JB right here." Chris was stumbling a little bit but still standing.

JB had on his jewelry as well, so he was shining like a rapper too, so the girls immediately flocked to him. One of the girls said, "Oooh he look fine, he the one they was talking 'bout?" The other girl replied, "Yeah but I think Mike got more money than him girl. You seen Mike new Benz?"

They were loud, rude and drunk.

"Chic you don't know what you talking about. JB got two cars, a Jag and a Lexus. My Dawg own his house, man my dawg used to move that weight."

The second girl replied, "Used to? Huh?"

One of the girls rubbed her booty up against JB. She said, "I wonder if he can still move..."

"Wait," JB said and backed up. Then replied, "Naw, I'm straight."

She leaned over to her friend and said, "Uh, oh girl he lame, that Nigga ain't no king pin. Let's go down there where Mike at. I need some weed to put with this Coke. I'm trying to smoke."

JB looked at Chris and said, "Man what you doing with them girls? They got you smoking that stuff. First you gone be smoking coke with weed, then you gone be smoking crack."

"Not, I ain't that stupid, I'll never do that."

JB told him, "I think you need to go to rehab."

'Bro you think if this stuff was beating me I would be able to make all this money? Chris pulled a stack of money out of his pocket, it was over $6500. "Dawg I got this, it ain't got me. Everybody just hating because 'they' can't handle it. Boy I been in love with drugs since a baby. I was smoking weed and drinking beer in my momma's stomach. I get all the money 'cause the girls love me, you see I had them until you ran them off. And guess what? I had all them in my bed last night and gone have even more in my bed tonight, now let's go party."

They partied and even convinced JB to take a drink. He managed to hold out for a whole two hours. But now everyone knows that temptation is hard to overcome, especially when you're around friends. Before he knew it four hours had passed and JB went from one beer to five beers, downed six shots and smoked three joints, and had a couple liquor in his hand.

It was coming up on 1:00 AM in the morning and JB knew Erica would be waiting. She would be angry that he was drunk but at least if he made it home safe that would be good enough. He could use the best friend birthday excuse and smooth talking to wiggle his way out of trouble.

Yet, the trouble that was approaching was going to take more than smooth talking to get out of.

JB, Chris, Mike, Chaz, Bruce and a lot of other folks were standing around JB's car talking about the old days. But JB had decided that it was time to go home. "Alright fellas, the reunion was nice but I must bounce. Happy birthday Mike boy, I'll catch you later."

Mike said, "Aww man the party ain't over yet fool. I still got a whole trunk full of liquor and more weed than California."

Then Chris chimed in, "Yep JB, you know you don't come around that much. Your girlfriend ain't gonna kill you."

One of the girls picking at JB said, "Oh so that's why the king pin was acting gay, he got a lil girlfriend."

Mike replied, "Naw this fool done got engaged on us, and he *was* the king pin. I'm the king pin now, and this is my city."

J3 turned to Mike and said, "Alright Mr. Mayor I'm gone, alright Chris make sure you wrap it up tonight."

Chris slapped the girl on the butt. "Oh I will don't worry.

The first girl said, "Wrap it up? Boy I ain't got nothing. Yo girl probably got something, you go home and you wrap it up fake kingpin. Go get in that old Jag and drive off, you just mad because Mike got a Benz and doing better than you."

JB should've just got in his car and left but his pride got the best of him... "Girl I don't care about no Benz. I don't care about how much money he got neither. I'm the one started this. Mike you better tell these the girls who put you on. If it wasn't for me, man it don't even matter. I know one thing, ya'll better tighten up.

Mike starting to get hot headed said, "Yeah but I made myself you ain't make me."

By this time they both were heated. JB said, "What!! I gave you and Chris everything that ya'll got."

Mike replied, "Naw you ain't give me this, I built this. Nigga I'm the one that paid for your lawyer."

"What!! Oh you really trippin now." Mike said, Naw I ain't trippin, if it wasn't for me you'd be doing 25 years. I had all that stuff gone in one day. You was even surprised at how fast it got moved. You couldn't have did it by yourself that fast and you know it, it was me. This jewelry me, this Benz me, this money me, this party me, nigga me. Nigga I can put you on now, you can come work for me on the block."

JB turned around and said, "So you gone disrespect me like that?" He walked toward Mike.

Chris stepped in between them, "No dawg ya'll break it up, ya'll boys."

"Disrespect you like what Nigga? You disrespecting yourself. Wanna come round here and think you better than us 'cause you go to church and you got you some little school girl. Nigga I can get 100 school girls, the problem is I ain't gone fall in love with no virgin like a sissy. Especially if I ain't never even had sex with her."

JB hit Mike and the two started fighting.

Chris tried to break it up but he was too drunk and he fell. Mike picked up a bottle off the ground and tried to hit JB with it but he ducked and it busted JB's passenger side window.

Some of Mike's new friends from the other side of town tried to jump in and help Mike beat up JB so Chaz and Bruce started fighting them off.

The whole party turned into chaos and a neighbor called the police. One of the boys that was on Mike's side pulled out a gun and started shooting. When the gun went off the crowd scattered. He tried to shoot Bruce but Chris grabbed him and he spun and hit a nearby woman in the chest.

It seemed like the police must have been right around the corner because they got there in less than three minutes.

The shooter threw his gun inside the broken window of JB's car and took off. Not knowing that the gun was in his car, JB jumped inside and started to drive away, but by that time it was too late. A police cruiser quickly swooped behind JB and two more officers were on foot running up to the car.

JB spotted the gun on the floor and threw it out of the window but it was too late. A police jumped in front of the car and aimed his gun right at JB's face. The other officer was standing right at the driver-side with his gun also. Two more police cruisers pulled up and they blocked off JB's car.

There was nowhere to run.

One of the officers told him to freeze and said, "Don't you move boy or I will shoot you dead right here."

JB did not move a muscle. He knew it was all over. Everything... his new life, his new job, his freedom, his friendship with Mike and most important of all, Erica.

The police picked up the shooter's gun which now had JB's fingerprints all over it and they snatched him out of the car. Everyone was gone, the street was deserted. Only four people remained, JB, the woman who got shot and her two friends who were trying to keep her alive until the paramedics arrived.

JB was all alone and on his way to jail.

Erica was at home worried sick about him, she had called his phone but got no answer. It was now 2:00am and she was tired.

She had to be at work by 6:00am.

Meanwhile JB had just gotten booked and was still trying to talk his way out of it. "I'm telling ya'll man, that ain't my gun. Somebody threw it in my car and I was trying to throw it out."

But there was no way the police was buying that story. They smelled alcohol on his breath and the weed on his clothes. They gave him a Breathalyzer test. He blew two times the legal limit. Because the car was actually in drive and moving when they stopped him, they charged him with DUI. What's worse is the fact that the woman was shot above the waist in the chest, so he also had a charge of attempted murder with a bond of $250,000.

It was not looking good at all, the only chance he had was if someone could come forward, testify and tell the police that he was not the shooter, but who was going to do that? Even if someone did there was no way the police was just going to open the door and just let him walk out.

He was back at square one, he had to bond out.

With no more product to sell that was not happening. The only person he knew that could help him was the one person who was somewhat responsible for him being there in the first place, Mike.

He had no choice but to call Erica, he didn't want to but he had to.

At 2:56am Erica got a phone call.

She jumped up to answer the phone because she knew it was JB, who else would be calling at that time. She didn't recognize the number so right away she feared something was wrong. When she answered and heard *"This is a free call from an inmate at the Pinellas County jail"* she dropped her head and immediately started crying.

When she pulled herself together the first thing she said was, "I told you, I told you, I told you but you wouldn't listen."

JB started talking fast and frantic. "Baby... baby no you gotta believe me I was on my way home and I was set up. I swear I didn't do nothing."

She could tell by his voice that he was drunk.

"And you've been drinking."

"Baby it was a party and yes I had something to drink but that's not important I need your help, I was set up. I need to get bonded out of here."

"I don't have any money. Plus I had a feeling this was going to happen, I'm done Jonathan."

"No baby please don't do this, it's not my fault you love me don't you, you just said that you would marry me. I need you to get me out."

"I promised myself that if you went back that I would not let you sweet talk me. Yes I love you but I can't and I won't risk my life for yours."

"You won't? Well I guess you don't know what marriage is 'cause I will not hesitate to risk my life for you. You know what, I don't blame you. You don't know anything about the struggle how it is to be down. You always been up. I always been down. I love you but..."

"But what Jonathan? But what? Say it."

145

"I'm not going to kiss your butt. If you don't believe me don't. If you want to leave go. All I'm asking you to do is help me get out of here before you leave. If you love me like you say you do at least do that."

"I can't believe this, what do I have to do?"

"First I need you to go under the mattress and get that $4,000. Then go to my mom's house and take her to get my car from the pound. It's in her name so they gonna give it to her with no problem. Then I need you to get the window fixed because Mike broke it."

'How did Mike break your window?"

"It's a long story, which is not important right now. After the window is fixed I need you to put both cars on Craig's List and sell them."

"Sell your cars why, how much is your bond?"

"You don't want to know. It's $250,000 baby."

Erica screamed. "$250,000? What the devil, why so much?"

"But I only need 10% so it's really just $25,000."

JB didn't want to say it but he spit it out. "Remember what I said, I didn't do this but they're charging me with attempted murder."

"Attempted murder!"

"Remember baby I didn't do it, I didn't do it. And once they talk to the girl and she says it wasn't me then I'll be good. It was a dude that was with Mike. He threw the gun into my car baby I swear I didn't do it. Matter of fact I know Chris will testify, and I know he'll tell the truth and help me out. And I'm not messing with Mike no more after this. It's all his fault the whole thing happened. He got drunk and started acting stupid. So can you please do this for me baby please?"

"I guess I don't have a choice do I?"

JB asked, "Hey ain't your mom a detective? Maybe she can help me out."

"Oh no, ain't no way I'm bringing my mom into this; plus she only investigates kidnappings, not murderers."

"Attempted murder baby."

"Whatever."

"Oh okay, so that's how she didn't know."

"Know what?"

"Oh nothing I was talking about something else."

"I can't believe this Johnathon, I don't think we should get married."

"Come on baby I can't handle all this right now I need my fiancée."

"No you don't because if you did you would have never left. Or you would have made sure you made it home. I don't care how stupid Mike acted, you are not Mike you are Jonathan. Look I have to be to work in three hours and I'm tired. I will help you when I get out of school. Or I will drop the money off to your mom after work and let her go get the car. I'll figure something out, but now I have to see how I can go to sleep with all this on my mind."

Before she got off the phone JB said, "Hey baby."

Sounding angry, tired and disappointed, she responded, "What Jonathan?"

"I love you."

"You sure have a weird way of showing it."

"Do you love me?"

"Yes, good night."

JB hung up the phone and a tear hit his eye. He couldn't believe he had just bought Erica a ring, proposed, she said yes and less than a week later he was back in jail for attempted murder.

He called Chris next.

He could only hope that he was still up and not passed out. The phone rung and Chris picked up it right away like he was already expecting the call. *"Hello."*

JB said, "Chris!"

*"JB what the hell man, I can't believe what just happened, bro I was high but that junk just made me sober, what happened? Why they took you to jail?"*

"Man, that nigga threw his gun in my car window that was broken, they got me in here on attempted murder bro. You know I didn't shoot that girl."

"Heck no, I saw what happened. I'm the one that was wrestling with that nigga."

"Bro you know I might need you to testify."

"Man don't trip I got you."

"But dawg you got to promise me you gone be able to control your habit man."

"Man listen I'll be up there in the morning when you go to advisory. I swear I got you."

"Chris man... I swear I ain't messing with Mike no more. I'm through with him."

Chris "Yeah that was messed up what he did, I don't blame you for that but damn, had no idea all that was gone happen."

"Man who was them other dudes that was with him?"

"Some dudes he's been hanging with. I think one of them is his baby mama brother."

"Okay well check this out I mean if you find out who that girl is tell her she got to tell the truth."

Chris clearing his throat, "Don't sweat it bro I already know who she is, she one of the chicks I had in my bed boy. I'm going to the hospital tomorrow. Don't worry you gone get out. How much you'll bond is bro?"

"$250,000, I mean $25,000."

"Dang I got some bread but nothing close to that. I can probably drop like $6000 to you."

"Will you dawg, you'll do that for me?"

"Man, you my Dawg, if it wasn't for you I would still be selling dime bags."

JB always spent more time with Mike and Chris was always like a shadow behind the two; yet right then JB knew that Chris was a real friend and Mike was a switch out.

JB said, "Man I appreciate it Chris I got to get out of here. And you all got to testify because I definitely don't have more money for another lawyer."

"Listen bro don't stress yourself out. You probably shouldn't have even come to the party but you did. I seen you trying to leave. Just like I saw you trying to get your life right. I know if I seen it God seen it. So I believe you gone be all right. You a good dude, you just got bad luck. Go to sleep or something chill out. Call me tomorrow bro."

"Okay man thank you Chris."

"JB you already know boy."

They hung up and JB thought about it. Chris really wasn't crazy. The dude actually sounded like he had some sense. JB tried to lie down and go to sleep but he couldn't. Even though he was in jail for attempted murder he knew he was innocent so that didn't bother him. The thing that bothered him was how his best friend since five years old could switch sides on him like that. He remembered the saying, *"The love of money is the root to all evil."*

He now knew it was true.

He also hated the fact that he had to let his new fiancée down. If stress caused gray hair he was about to grow a head full in one night.

He forced himself to sleep.

Chris came the next day just like he said would. Erica was also there. She called out of work to be there for him.

Chris told the judge that JB was not the shooter but without the victim herself who was still in the hospital present, saying the same thing, he didn't care to hear Chris' statement.

For all he knew he could have been anybody.

All Erica could do was tell the judge what JB told her. She also added that her fiancé was a good man who just happened to be in the wrong place at the wrong time.

After court was over Chris went to the hospital and Erica went to JB's mother's house. Erica did everything JB had instructed her to do and she put both of the cars on Craig's List. JB told her to sell the Jaguar for $20,000 and the Lexus for $15,000.

Chris was able to get the victim to agree to testify that JB was not the shooter and that the shooter was still on the streets. Although she made the statement, the detective still decided to do a full investigation to make sure what she was saying was true and that she hadn't been threatened into making a false report.

So that kept JB in jail for a little while longer. That and the fact that not one person seemed interested in buying either car.

He talked to Erica every day, and every day she would say no one said anything. She suggested that he cropped the price a little. The Jaguar was a 2010, the value was nowhere near $20,000 even with the chrome rims, TVs and music system.

The Lexus was overpriced too.

The 2004 Lexus was only worth about $8,000 with the miles it had on it. He told her to change both of them, put $12,000 for the Jag, $7,000 for the Lexus and with the $6000 that Chris would give him he would be able to get out.

The following day she had a buyer for the Lexus but still not one hit on the Jaguar. A whole month passed and the arraignment court date had been set for JB. He also just received the court date for the first shooting from the convenience store.

He knew he had to get out and get out quick.

Meanwhile, the police had caught up with the real shooter but wasn't going to let JB go without knowing for sure who was responsible. With JB's prints on the gun and others saying someone else was the shooter it was a toss-up.

JB was not going to get out of this easy. He was in deep trouble but he knew he had to fight since he was not the shooter.

JB knew he could take it to trial and probably win, but most murder trials take anywhere from one to three years, maybe longer.

And he just didn't have that kind of time.

Then one day out of nowhere, Erica got a hit on her laptop while at school. She had a buyer for the Jag. She met the buyer after school got the money and JB was bonded out three hours later.

A whole month and four days had passed and JB was finally back face to face with his fiancée. He was so excited to see Erica. "Baby I'm so happy to see you, thank you so much for getting me out."

"You're welcome. Your mom had to put up the house for collateral."

"Yeah I know. I miss my cars already but I'm just glad to be out. Man forget those cars I miss *you* so much."

"I miss you too."

"I got to go thank my boy Chris too."

"No, you're not going anywhere Mr. you can call him on the phone if you want to. Or he can come to you but you're not leaving my sight. I got you all to myself."

She didn't know that JB had two weeks before he was to turn himself back in and start his two year sentence. He had a scheduled appointment with the lawyer, he asked JB to come into the office, and he said it was urgent.

"JB, the judge gave us the two year deal. But he said only if you take it now. If you wait and put it off it is going to be five or maybe ten, he wants an answer by tomorrow.

JB had no choice but to sign the plea deal.

Erica was hurt but she knew it was coming eventually so she was prepared for it.

"Baby I know you're mad but you're not madder than me, I'm the one that has to do the time. If I can do it I know you can."

"Two years is a long time Johnathon."

"Baby if you just work and focus on school this will all be over before you know it. And I swear it'll just be me and you. No Mike, no Chris, no parties... nothing. I love you and I need you."

"I love too."

JB called Chris and thanked him for everything he did. He told him about the upcoming prison sentence and his plans for Erica when he got out. He wished him luck and that was the last time he talked to Chris.

Those two weeks went by and Erica dropped him back off at the jailhouse. While he was in jail more witnesses came forward about the party shooting and it eventually led to him being acquitted of all charges, all except the DUI.

Things weren't going so good for the real shooter though. He was charged with attempted murder and given the same bond as JB but had no house or cars to sell to get out so he was stuck. He really didn't have much, he was just a hot headed kid trying to make a name for himself. Someone Mike hired to stick by his side just in case something went down. Someone who wasn't afraid to get his hands dirty.

Something like a security guard, slash hitman.

Mike paid him $1000 a week to make sure no other drug dealers, or anybody for that matter got in the way of his money.

But now he was about to get sixty years because his record was ten times worse than JB's. There was one problem though, there were two at the party. Mike had another security guard slash, hitman still out there. He was the cousin of the shooter.

Another hot headed $1,000 a week flunky.

His name was Red and he wasn't too happy about his cousin getting locked up. He strongly believed in the popular saying "snitches get stitches."

About two months after police had finished their investigation Red decided to do some investigating of his own. He set out on a mission to find Chris and make sure that he would never tell on any one else ever again. Unlike his cousin, Red was smart, he didn't just go around shooting people. He was more on the sneaky side.

He followed Chris to a bar one night. He waited for Chris to get drunk and go to the bathroom. He went in after him and attacked him. After Chris was on the floor dazed and confused he pulled out two syringes. He injected Chris with the first one which was filled with heroin and then injected him with the second one which was filled with blood containing the AIDS virus.

He whispered in Chris's ear, "Hey man try this, its heroin. It's ten times better than Cocaine." He disappeared leaving Chris on the floor.

It was a small dose of heroin so Chris was back on his feet within minutes but it was more than enough to make a first time user feel one hell of a rush.

When Chris came out of the bathroom he wanted more. It just so happened that he was at the right bar, and with a pocket full of money he could get whatever he wanted.

It was time for Red to go after his next victim. He went down the line of witnesses that testified or anyone who had anything to do with anyone who knew what went down that night at the party. Sitting at the end of the lists of names was 'Starbucks'.

He remembered hearing Mike talk about how his friend JB had betrayed him over some virgin who worked at Starbucks. He didn't know her name but he had ways of finding out, and he did.

One day he went to Starbucks and sat in the parking lot with the pair of binoculars. He had a good close-up of Erica. He didn't know exactly how he wanted to make her pay, but all he knew is that she was going to pay. He saw that she was pretty so he thought about raping her but no, he wanted to do something to send a bigger message to JB.

He stayed till she got off and followed her home.

He watched as she got out of the car and as soon as she opened the door to the house he ran in after. He beat her up then tied her up. He told her, "You will never see JB again Starbucks, and he will never see you either."

Red set the house on fire with Erica tied up inside. He thought that the house would burn down and that would be his justice for his cousin but he was wrong.

Erica's mom taught her a few things about kidnappers. She taught her how to hold her hands just in case she was ever tied up. So Erica was able to get free almost immediately after Red ran out of the door. She watched out the window as he ran to his car and drove off.

She was not able to put the fire out, it had grown too fast. Erica ran out the door and screamed for help but no one heard her.

She drove to the closest place she knew she could be safe, JB's mom's house. From there, she called 911 and explained everything that happened. She cried to Cynthia about how much she loved JB and how much she tried to stick with him but after that, there was no way she could stay.

Cynthia tried to talk her out of it but Erica had made up her mind. She had moved her whole apartment into JB's home, and now everything was on fire. She lost everything she had that day, including her love. She left the ring with Cynthia and she left so that she could go file a report with the police and get treated for her injuries.

She called her mom to let her know what was going on, still crying and in shock she made up her mind that day that she was not taking him back this time.

She'd had enough.

Back in prison JB had no idea what was going on outside of the prison walls. He went to call Erica that evening like he normally did at 6:30 pm after school, but he got no answer. He tried again still no answer. He kept trying and trying but got nothing.

He called his mom to see if she had heard from her. When Cynthia told him what happened his heart stopped, he could hardly catch his breath. He cried and cried, he begged his mom to go get her back. He asked her to talk to Erica but Cynthia told him she had already said all she could say, Erica was gone and she had left the ring.

All the stress and drama, confusion and chaos and everything was just too much for her, she started feeling chest pains. She called his name... *Jonathan*...

but JB was so busy crying and talking loud and carrying on he couldn't hear.

She said it again as loud as she could with all her breath... "Jonathan!"

That time he heard her. "Yes ma'am."

She said, "Call somebody I think am having another heart attack."

There was a silence on the phone for a second, then he heard the phone hit the floor first and his mom hit the floor after that.

He had no time to call anyone else collect and hope they'd answer, that would take too long, and he had to move fast.

He screamed for the guards.

The guard came. "Help. My Momma just had a heart attack on the phone. Please, you have to get the ambulance to 921 24th St. South. I'm serious I'm not joking."

The next couple of minutes were the longest and scariest minutes of JB's life. Not knowing what was going on was killing him inside. He was about to have a heart attack himself. The guard came back and told him not to worry help was on the way.

J3 hit rock-bottom that day. He was in prison, he lost his two cars, his house, his best friend, his fiancée and now his mother just had a second heart attack.

He literally had nothing left, *nothing* but God.

# CHAPTER 6

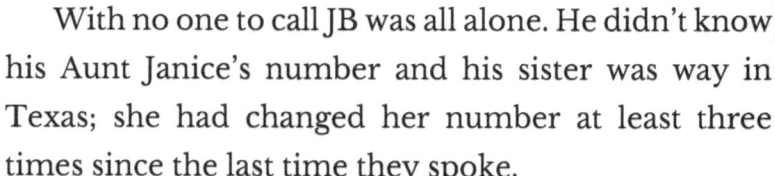

With no one to call JB was all alone. He didn't know his Aunt Janice's number and his sister was way in Texas; she had changed her number at least three times since the last time they spoke.

He tried calling Chris but even his number was disconnected.

He had been in prison going on two months now and had not gotten one single visit. He was breaking down inside. He'd done time before but this particular time was different. All he could think about was how he messed up.

He never thought about changing his life so he never tried. Then the one time he goes and tries...

things fail. He let his mother down and let Erica down and he let himself down.

He walked around with an attitude all the time, he barely spoke to anyone. Guys he knew on the street would try to strike up conversations about the old days but he wasn't interested in going down memory lane.

He was not proud of the things he had done, the life he had lived. He felt it was a waste of time, all for nothing. Sure he had fun but a little fun ain't worth a lot of pain, right? All those years of hustling on the corners, making drop-offs, serving large amount of drugs and dodging police just wasn't worth it in the end. He had nothing to show for the stuff he did and the money he made.

Those thoughts made him even madder and he began not to care anymore. Instead of moving forward he was falling backwards, and fast.

He got into two fights and was sent to the box for thirty days. Inside prison your freedom is gone but inside the box everything is gone. You get no phone calls, no mail, no commissary and no TV.

Now with no one to communicate with at all he began to read the Bible every day and talk to God. He often asked God questions like *"Why me?" "Why do I fail even when I try to do the right thing?" "Will I ever make it out of this suffering?"*

Although he read the Bible a couple times a day, he didn't really understand a lot of what he read.

He started to feel like there was no use.

Breaking down into tears and crying, he wished that he never would've hit Mike that night at the party. He began wishing he had never gone to the party at all. He wish he had never sold drugs, he even wished that he had never been born.

He was at the lowest point of his life.

At that very moment JB thought about suicide. *Would anybody miss me if I was gone?* That was the question he asked himself. He wondered would anyone even care. He thought about how many people would actually take the time to show up at his funeral. *Would it be big or small? Would Erica come? And would she cry?*

So many things went through JB's mind it was a good thing he only had 30 days; something like three to six months would have driven him crazy. That 30<sup>th</sup>

day finally came in and he was released from the box and sent back to regular population.

That's when he found that he had two letters waiting on him, both from his older sister in Texas.

In the first letter she told him that his mother was alright. After her 2nd heart attack she spent 2 weeks in the hospital but was now back at home.

It was a short letter, she spoke mostly about their mom and that was it. The second letter that came just two days before he was released from the box was a little longer. His sister told him that the tumors the doctors removed had come back and even worse, had turned into cancer. She went on about how their mother had been doing fine until worrying about his lifestyle put a tremendous amount of pressure on her.

Basically she blamed JB for his mother's two heart attacks, and it sounded like she was blaming him for her cancer as well.

JB was furious and ripped up the letter and cursed his sister. He immediately got on the phone and called his mom. They talked about her health and he apologized again for how he had caused so much stress on her.

She told him that although he had put her under a lot of stress not to blame himself because whatever happened it was meant to happen. She reminded him that she still loved him and would always love him. The only thing she was mad at him about was the fact that he had so much potential but didn't do anything with it.

All she wanted him to do was get his life in order.

He asked her if she had heard anything from Erica and she said, "No."

Disappointed by her response, that put an even bigger dent in his heart. He couldn't believe it... not one letter, no phone call; she didn't even stop by and ask how he was doing or anything.

When the phone call was over JB tried to call Erica but her number had been disconnected. One day while at the nurses office for a checkup JB stepped out on the scale and notice that he had lost twenty-eight pounds, he was in bad shape.

He barely ate, he barely talked; honestly, he hardly did anything at all besides sleep.

He had given up on life.

One night while lying in bed he said three simple words *"Jesus help me."* He gave everything he had over to the Lord.

That's when God began to work in his life.

The next morning JB woke up to the loud banging of the cell door closing. It was the guard bringing in a new inmate. JB heard him say, "Okay Mr. Trudi go easy on him."

JB had spent almost three weeks by himself since his last roommate went home. As the old gray haired white man entered the room JB stared him up and down thinking to himself, *"oh lord here goes somebody else I'm not going to get along with."* JB threw his cover over his face and turned over facing the wall. He said to the old man, "don't be making a lot of noise and don't step on my bed when you go to the top."

JB went back to sleep. Two hours later when JB woke up he saw the old man sitting at the table reading his Bible. The old man turned towards JB and said in a joking kind of way, "My reading wasn't too much noise for you was it?"

With a smirk on his face JB said, "No I just couldn't sleep no more, I think I'm all slept out."

"Yeah, I know what you mean I've been like that a few times."

Mr. Trudi extended his arm out to greet JB with a handshake, "Hey nice to meet you my name is Ben or Mr. Trudi, that's what everyone else calls me."

JB shook his hand and said, "They call me JB."

"Well JB looks like you're my last stop."

"Huh, what you mean by that?" JB looked confused, then he thought about what the guard said earlier. *"Okay Mr. Trudi go easy on him." Is this man old man a serial killer or something, why would the guards say that?*

Mr. Trudi recognized JB's confused look and said, "You're my last stop, unless they come up with a clever idea to move me again. I'm going home in 6 months."

"Oh yeah, how long you been in here?"

"Aww I don't know, somewhere around thirty-nine years, six months, three days and a couple of hours I guess."

JB's jaw dropped.

"Thirty-nine years!! For what?"

"Oh they said I robbed some banks."

"And you saying you didn't do it?"

"No ... I did it, but that wasn't me, this is me. What about you, how long have you been here, when do you get out?"

"Almost three months, I got two years."

"Oh, that's nothing you'll be fine."

"Yeah right man, I can't take it. I don't see how you did 39 years I probably would have killed myself."

"Oh ... believe me at first it was hard, but it takes a whole lot and I mean a whole lot of God. He's the only way I made it as long as I did. Oh yeah and I did kill myself. Do you know God?"

Daydreaming a little bit JB missed the part when Mr. Trudi said he killed himself. "Yeah, I know God a little bit, I was going to church with my fiancée before I came here."

"How much is a little bit? Do you have a personal relationship with him?"

"Ummm yeah kind of, I was about to but like I said I came in here."

"Well coming in here doesn't stop anything. Whatever you did on the streets you can do in here. You can read your Bible, talk to Him, pray to Him, go to church and you can even be baptized and born again. Prison doesn't stop your relationship with God. That's the only thing the guards can't take away from you. They can take any and everything but they can't take God.

How do you think I made it this long? Jesus freed me. I'm free within myself. Handcuffs, walls, bars, the box, nothing can change that. It's all in here and here (as he points to his head and heart)."

"So when you read the Bible you know what you be reading, you can understand it?"

"Of course, see the key is to read the whole book. Not the whole Bible but when I say the whole book, I mean like *Mark, Matthew, Luke, John*. Those are books inside the Bible. When you read, read the whole book, that works best for me. A lot of people just jump around from page to page, Scripture to scripture and really have no idea what they're reading. When you read the whole book, say for instance 1st Kings it tells you a story. You get to learn who the characters are and what they did. How God blessed them and how God punished them.

I always thought that the Bible was a boring book. Really I didn't know what to think because I never took the time to find out. But once I got deep into it I really started to understand it, I came to see that believe it or not it's rather interesting. You can learn a lot from the Bible."

JB responded, "Yeah I gotta learn how to read it because I gotta change my life."

"What? Let me be the first to tell you it is never too late. Just know that the Bible doesn't change your life though. You change your life, it just gives you instructions on how to do it. It's not a magic book, you have to do the work.

Listen here, I go to the religious service meeting every Wednesday, if you want to go all you have to do is sign up."

"Yeah, I think that's what I'm gonna do 'cause I need to get around some positive people. Everybody around here is negative, not you, but mostly 90% of the people in prison. I already got enough bad luck as it is."

Mr. Trudi, teaching JB at this point said, "No sir there is no such thing as bad luck."

JB looked at him sideways and said, "Yeah right."

"No, it's true, when you do the right thing good things happen, when you do the wrong thing bad things happen. Much of our life we control with the decisions we choose to make. A wise man learns from his mistakes, but a fool continues to do the same thing over and over. A mistake is only a mistake if you don't know you're making it. If you already know it is wrong then it is not a mistake, you're just testing the waters to see if you can get away with it.

I'm sure you did something to get locked up, you didn't just wake up one morning and the judge decided to slap you in the face with two years. There had to be a time where you had a yes or no decision right in front of you. Saying no was just as easy as saying yes but you chose yes and now you're in here. No would've had you at home with your family, am I wrong?"

"No you're absolutely right, all I had to do was get in the car and drive away. Now my fiancée gone... she left me, she won't even answer the phone. We probably would have been married by now."

Mr. Trudi saw how down JB looked whenever he talked about Erica. "Don't worry you'll get her back, if she *really* loves you, she hasn't went far. If she did then I don't know what to say, I don't have all the answers. I do know one thing though, even if you can't get her back God can. Just pray on it and ask God to make you a better man.

You have twenty months to become transformed, so when you get out of here and step in front of her she'll see a new man. But don't just do it for her, change because you want to change, because it's the right thing to do. God is a jealous God... you can't put anything before Him, not even her.

This is what you have to remember, God 1st everything else 2nd, everything. Do that and watch how different your life becomes. You'll find a peace that you never thought could be found.

That's how someone like me survived as long as I did in here. I've had every kind of car I ever wanted, partied like a rock star, slept with some of the most beautiful women on earth and had in my possession over $1 million in cash, I lost it all. I traveled around the world just to land here and spend 39 years in an 8 x 10 cell. I had a son in high school and I haven't seen him since he was 3 and that was 51 years ago.

I should be bald from pulling my hair out. Instead I'm happier than I've ever been and it is all because of the good Lord. That's exactly why I say it is never too late. Through Christ all things are possible."

JB felt encouraged after talking to and listening to Mr. Trudi. He started reading the Bible more and more. Sometimes he would read with Mr. Trudi sometimes he would read alone.

He also prayed a lot more and asked God to show him the things he couldn't see before; things like how to spot the tricks of the devil.

He prayed for wisdom, strength, understanding, knowledge and humbleness. He signed up with the prison's church service, and when he went he always asked a lot of questions. For the next month he studied the Bible like he was preparing for a test.

JB called his mom every two days to check on her. She was now taking chemotherapy and starting to lose her hair.

The months weren't going by fast enough for JB.

He wanted to be there for her, he prayed and prayed that God would take her cancer away. Even though she was sick she still had that great sense of humor. They talked and laughed like they had always done in the past. She'd tell him how Mr. Ru from across the street had been fighting with his wife because he wouldn't stop flirting with the young girls in the neighborhood.

And JB told her how funny Mr. Trudi looked when he worked out, a man in his 70s trying to do push-ups was just the funniest thing ever to him.

It seemed like Mr. Trudi was right about what he said though. When you give everything to God it takes a lot of pressure off.

He didn't worry about the things he couldn't control anymore. A few more weeks went by and JB had reached the four month mark. He still kept to himself a lot. He still never played cards or went out to the Rec yard. Whenever he worked out it was in his room and he only talked to a few people like Mr. Trudi and some other guys from the church service; he was really sticking to his word.

He was determined to change, he wasn't focused on anything but that. That and getting his girl back.

He thought about Erica all the time, so many things ran through his mind. *Was she thinking about him? Was she missing him? Was she seeing someone else? Did she love him or did she hate him? Would she ever talk to him again? Was she gone for good or would she see his change, forgive him and take him back?*

JB still hadn't heard from Erica but it didn't matter whether she loved him or not, he loved her and that was enough for him. There was no way he was going to give up until he stood face-to-face with her and watched her walk away, only then would he let her go without putting up a fight.

JB knew she had every right to be pissed off at him. It was because of him she got beat up and lost everything she had. If it had not been for her attacker's inability to tie a good knot, she would have lost her life that day in the fire.

There was so many things JB was guilty of, so many sins he had committed.

He said a special prayer, repented and asked for forgiveness: *Dear Lord it is me your son. Today I come to you in Jesus name asking for forgiveness. I am a sinner and I lived my life the wrong way. I did a lot of bad things that I knew wasn't right. But I'm so sorry, I don't even deserve to live but I'm here so I thank you. Now I'm on a new path and I want to live better. I only want to live for you. Please forgive me for everything I've done that you didn't approve of. Let your light shine on me Lord. Give me back everything I lost. And please let my mom beat this cancer. In Jesus name I pray Amen.*

Mr. Trudi asked him, "So how do you feel now?"

"Huh? What you mean?"

Every now and then Mr. Trudi would randomly ask JB pop up questions, things like "Who are you?" "Would you do nothing again?" "What's better, to live to die or to die to live?"

Mr. Trudi had a crazy way of talking sometimes but it always made sense, so again he asked JB, "How do you feel now?"

"Ummm, I feel good, well kind of good. I'm better than I was when I first came in. I still can't wait to go home though."

"Yeah I know, that feeling never goes away. Anyone who wants to stay here is nuts. But no, what I'm saying is do you feel like a Christian yet?"

"I don't know what a Christian is supposed to feel like. I feel different though."

"That's good but when you're a Christian you feel more than different, you feel funny. You start to feel strange, weird, out of place like you are not even in your body sometimes. The same things don't get your attention anymore. You start to hate the things you once loved. You'll talk different too, like when you say a curse word it'll feel wrong. You'll start to try to catch yourself more and more till one day you won't curse at all. You'll stop being selfish.

Before if a person on the street asked for a dollar, you would keep walking and not think nothing of it, once you are a Christian little things like that get to you. You might keep walking but it eats at your conscience till you turn around and give that dollar.

Then the next time you might not even walk away, as soon as they ask you give. Don't be surprised if one day you find yourself giving before they get a chance to ask. Those are the kind of signs that let you know you are a Christian. When doing the right thing becomes normal and even fun, when before it was uncool and lame. You know you're a Christian when you become the same person you used to make fun of and talk about.

See when you're living wrong, it works the same way but only down. You get better and better at becoming bad. Kind of like the people in here, prison is a college for criminals. They get better and better until they fall down two ways, life in here or death out there. Christians get better and better the right way which is up, there's no stopping. You just grow and grow and grow. A Christian becomes wiser and wiser, smarter and smarter, loves more and more until they go to Heaven.

And even then it doesn't stop. You go on and on living the good life, happiness forever and ever. Who doesn't want that right?"

JB responded, "Hmm you'll be surprised."

"Yeah I know and it's sad. I see fellas come and go, then come and go again, the same ones. I've talked to at least 300 or more different men, old and young. That's why the guards tell me to go easy. I've had roommates kick me out of their rooms, I've had others leave their own rooms. I've had guys threaten to bash my head in if I kept talking about Jesus.

There's something special about you son, you listen well. I can tell you want it. Yes... I can tell because a lot of fellas I've seen run from this word like a wild lion was chasing them in the jungle. If you want to run somebody off in a hurry just keep talking about Jesus.

Boy you'll see them high tail it so fast, I'm telling you they don't want to hear it. Oohwee the devil hates God. Oh and that's another thing JB, being a Christian comes with lumps on your head. You can't be no punk sissy if you want to be a child of the King.

The closer you try to get to God the more that devil is gonna whoop up on you boy like you stole something. There's always going to be some kind of test, wall, obstacle or something trying to come between you and God. It's gonna be hard, because staying a Christian sometimes it's harder than becoming one in the first place, really about the hardest thing you ever had to do, but don't give up."

"I ain't gonna give up. I just can't wait to get baptized next week."

"Yeah that's when you get born again. But that water don't change you, you can get baptized and kill someone ten minutes later. So the water don't change you, you change you. It just makes you born again. You become a new creature in Christ. The old you dies and the new you is born. You stay in this world but you don't live in this world, you live in the spirit. Everything you do, every step you take you let the Holy Spirit guide you."

"Mr. Trudi you could be a preacher, you sound just like one."

They both laughed.

JB took everything Mr. Trudi had taught him and tucked away in his head and heart. He was baptized the following week and became born again.

When JB first started out on the streets he didn't know the first thing about being a thug. He had to learn how to fight, how to con folks, how to sell drugs and how to pimp women. He made a big name for himself and lived a pretty comfortable life too.

Mr. Trudi said being a Christian was going to be the hardest thing he ever had to do, well he didn't think anything could be harder than the life he had just left. If he could learn to be a thug, he could learn to be a Christian.

All through school he was very competitive, he hated to lose and he never backed down from a challenge. Once he made up his mind to do something, it was going to get done, oh yeah he was going to do it.

He told his mom about how he was reading the Bible and going to the religious services and trying to change, but everyone reads the Bible when they go to jail... even she knew that.

However, what she didn't know because JB wanted to keep it a surprise, is that he was going to be baptized. Although he did go to church with his grandmother when he was little he never got baptized. He thought that little bit of good news might cheer his mom up while she was dealing with her cancer.

So he picked up the phone and called her.

She moved a slight bit slower than she did before the cancer so the phone rang a couple more times than usual, but he wasn't worried she always picked up.

*"Hello."*

"Hey mom, how you doing today?"

*"Oh, I'm hanging in there son... just sitting here watching my stories and watching Mr. Ru through the window."*

"Oh yeah what that crazy fool doing over there?"

*"Well I guess he tried to rake the yard but it looked like the rake put a beating on him."*

JB replied, "Yeah he getting old, but one thing I can say is that he got the greenest grass on the block."

*"Yeah I should tell him to let me have it when he die."*

"Ma, now you know that God don't like ugly."

*"Yeah I know, and right about now a lady like me need all the blessings I can get."*

"Oh yeah, well I just so happen to have a blessing for you mom, I got baptized today."

*"Oh really that's nice, real nice Jonathan I'm so proud of you, maybe now you will try to act right."*

"Oh Naw ain't no try, me and Mr. Trudi been studying every day. I be going hard now Momma, I'm on my way. The old me has died, the new me has risen, I'm a born again, Christian now."

In all her life Cynthia never heard her son talk like that, she was shocked and not sure if she believed him, but happy all at the same time.

*"Now you sound like somebody, not the Johnathon I know. God must have answered both of our prayers because I have some good news for you too."*

JB thought that his mom was going to say there was a turnaround in the cancer.

"For real... what? Is your cancer leaving?"

*"Oh no I wish, but it's not that. I was at the grocery store with your Auntie Janice and I ran into Erica."*

JB's eyes got big like he heard the guards say roll it up Griffin you're going home.

"Swear!! Oh my God what she said, what she said?"

*"Well she was coming out while we were going in. She was with her mom and she just spoke to me. I didn't even see her she saw me. She said, 'hey' and asked how you was doing. I said, 'he's fine' and that you are going to church inside there. Then she asked how I was doing and I told her about the cancer. She said she would check up on me from time to time when she could because she was real busy with school."*

"That's it, that's all she said?"

*"Yeah that's all she said, you hurt that girl, and I could see it all over her face. But I could also see that she missed you."*

"Oh yeah, how you seen that?"

*"Because when I said you was alright she kind of smiled a little bit. Then when I said you be asking about her every time you call she smiled again."*

"Oh yeah, you told her that?"

*"You know I had to put a little word in there for you."*

"Thanks mom, that's what's up," JB yelled. "Yes, that's what I'm talking 'bout, my Momma a OG."

*"No I just don't want to see you suffering. Even though you deserve everything you got, you are my only son and I love you. And I know you love her."*

"Did she say she still love me?"

*"She didn't say that, but I know she do. Love just don't disappear like that."*

"Hey Momma, do me a favor please?"

*"What boy I ain't fenna be chasing that girl for you, you got to go do your own chasing now."*

"Naw Ma listen, all I want you to do is do this, where you put the ring at?"

*"It's in my dresser? Shoot I thought about pawning it and getting me some money, that thing so pretty. No I'm just playing, but it is pretty though."*

"Hey Ma listen, when she come over there to check up on you, I want you to put it on the coffee table in the living room. And when she see it you tell her that it ain't moved since the day she gave it back. Tell her I said it is gonna stay right there until she decide she want it back, and when she want it... she can have it."

*"Boy who you think you is? I tell you one thing, you are like your daddy."*

"Ma you gone do it? You gone do that for me?"

*"And what you gone do for me?"*

"Momma, don't do me like that, I already changed my life."

*"Boy that ain't for me that's for you. Because that is what you need to do. That's between you and God."*

"Mom please, I got you I promise."

*"Whatever boy."*

JB finished talking to his mom until the call was over. When he went back to the cell Mr. Trudi knew by the pep in JB's step that he heard something good.

"You got your girl back?"

"I didn't get her back but my momma said she seen her and she asked about me." JB was happier than he had been in a long time. As a matter of fact he hadn't been that happy since the day he last saw her.

"You thank Him?"

There was another pop-up question JB wasn't ready for.

'Huh?"

"Did you thank God for answering your prayers?"

"Oh no, 'thank you, thank you, thank you, thank you Jesus, thank you Jesus, thank you Jesus.' But he didn't bring her back, she just asked about me."

"But that's a start son. God answers prayers the way He wants to answer them, not the way you want. When you learn that you'll get a better understanding of how to pray. He's not going to just drop everything in your lap. Then you might forget about Him. He gives it to you in pieces sometimes. So you can know it's Him and nobody but Him. So you can praise Him and give Him the glory and not yourself."

"You right. I'm just so happy, I hope she come to see me." Yet Erica didn't come see him, she didn't even make it over to his mom's house until three weeks later. When she did show up she only stayed about ten minutes and she left without the ring.

JB asked his mom to do all sorts of things to try and win Erica back. He asked his mom to cook dinner and try to get her to stay longer. He asked if she could get her to leave a phone number or address to where she was staying but she said she wasn't really ready to talk. She made it clear that she was only there to check up on Cynthia.

JB felt himself falling back into a depressive state but he didn't crumble, he just prayed more often and harder. Time seemed to pass quickly and now JB had been in prison for about five months and he still had not heard from the love of his life.

Then one day it happened, JB called his mom like he always did at story time. The phone rung and someone picked it up but it wasn't his mother.

It was a voice he hadn't heard in a long time. It was Erica.

*"Hello..."*

When JB heard Erica's voice come through that phone it was like a bolt of energy came with it. An electrical shock carrying the feelings of love, joy, happiness, peace, freedom and satisfaction all bottled up into one super emotion - it had to come from heaven.

"Hey baby. I waited so long for this, thank you Jesus."

Erica heard a difference in his voice, not because they hadn't spoken in five months but because the way he talked was calmer, more mature and more humble.

*"How are you doing in there Jonathan?"*

"Oh, I'm okay, hanging in there taking it one day at a time. I tell you what though, I'm feeling great now that I'm talking to you. I felt like this the whole time I've been in here. So what got you on the phone today?"

*"Umm, Jonathan I can't lie and say I don't miss you 'cause I do. I just wanted to hear your voice. I just had to wait until I was ready. Your mom told me you got baptized and you was really taking your walk with God serious."*

"Yep and it's all because of you, I mean I'm doing it for myself and for God, but you are the one who introduced me back to the church. Baby... I miss you so much and I'm sorry; if you, just take me back ..." Erica stopped him from saying anything else. She just wasn't ready for him to talk about reconciliation.

THE BROKEN CHAIN REACTION

*"Jonathan don't do that right now please I didn't get on the phone..."*

JB interrupted "... so you saying you don't love me no more? Doesn't the Bible say forgive?"

Erica was silent for a second. *"Yes, I love you and yes it says that. I already forgave you, but that doesn't mean I have to take you back. I had nothing left but my laptop and my car everything else is gone. I had to hear a forty-five day lecture from my mom. All my friends told me how stupid I was. I had to get money from my mom to buy all new clothes and everything.*

*I had to get stitches.*

*Jonathan I almost got burned to death in a fire. Please tell me what love has to do with any of that?"*

"Baby you're right. And I know you probably don't even want me to call you baby but that's how I feel. I never stop thinking about you, never. I replay everything over and over in my mind. I constantly ask God to erase it but it's still there. I can't change what happened yesterday and I can't even promise that it won't happen again tomorrow.

What I can promise though, is that for the rest of my life I will live for God and only God. I will be the best Christian I can be. I gave my life to GOD and now God orders my footsteps. I won't be perfect but I will be light years away from the man you left. If you fell for him and agreed to marry him then you will be 10 times happier with the new me.

I know that you still busy with school, how is that going for you?"

*"It's good, I still have a long way to go, when everything happened I fell behind a lot, I couldn't focus."*

"I'm so sorry boo, and I know you super busy trying to catch up but if it's not too much to ask I really, really, really would like to see you again."

The phone gave that 1 minute remaining warning.

Erica responded, *"I don't know about that."*

"Well, can I at least talk to you again? Can I write you or something?"

*"Oh no! I'm living with my mom and if she sees a letter from the jail with your name on it I won't hear the end of it."*

"Well when are you going to see my mom again?"

*"I don't know."*

"Well when you leave are you going to take your ring?"

*"No Jonathan I'm not taking the ring."*

"Baby..."

*"It was nice talking to you Jonathan. I have to go."*

"Baby..."

Erica starts to cry. *"Bye Jonathan."*

JB starts to cry also. "Baby, I love you (the phone hangs up)."

JB wanted to call back but there were other inmates in line waiting to use the phone. He was devastated. Happy he got a chance to talk to her but hurt that it didn't go the way he wanted it to.

Erica was in tears and confused too. She didn't know what to do. She didn't know whether she had made a mistake by speaking to Cynthia at the grocery store and stopping by her house or what.

Did she make the mistake of talking to him?

She wondered should she had just gone on with her life like she was or was that supposed to happen. Was she going off her own mind or was God sending her in that direction? She stayed there and cried.

Cynthia came over to comfort her. They sat and talked for almost thirty minutes after that. The whole time Erica waited for the phone to ring yet it never did.

Cynthia got up to use the bathroom and Erica just sat there staring at the ring. Erica told JB's mom, "You know what I think I'm just going to go. I'll see you later Ms Cynthia. Do you need anything before I go?"

Cynthia yelled from the bathroom, "No baby thank you anyways, just make sure you lock that door when you leave."

"Okay see you later."

"Okay bye sweetie."

Erica locked the door and left. When Cynthia came out of the bathroom she sat down to watch the rest of her stories. The ring was gone and there was a small note on the table. It read *please tell JB to call me* and it had a phone number.

Back at the prison JB didn't say anything for a while, he just stared at the wall until he fell asleep.

Mr. Trudi thought about trying to talk to him because he knew when JB had something on his mind, but he just minded his business that day and left JB to himself.

It wasn't long and JB was back to normal. He told himself that he wasn't going to beat himself up anymore. He let go and let God and said if he was going to trust God he was going to trust Him all the way and that's what he did.

Another day passed and it was time for JB to call his mom again. He called her and before she told him about the ring and the letter she had a little heart-to-heart talk with him. She told him about life and second chances. About being smart and being hardheaded. About surviving and living life. She knew the 20 minute call was about to be over so she said, *"Before I go I want to tell you this, are you listening?"*

"Yes ma'am."

*"That girl Erica is a good girl, I told you that when you first met her. She sat here and cried on my shoulder. I like her a lot and I will be happy to have her as a daughter-in-law. You better thank the good Lord above that He put her in your life. She's special so you better mean every word when you talk about being a Christian.*

*Because you can play with me and you can play with Erica but you can't play with Him now.*

*"Write this number down so you can call your fiancée."*

**196**

"What!! She gave you the number? Did she take the ring?"

*"Yes Jonathan she took the ring."*

JB thanked the Lord, thanked his mom, thanked the guards, he thanked the phone company and gave Mr. Trudi a big hug when he got back to the cell.

A couple hours later he called Erica, they talked and laughed, cried and laughed some more. She'd told him that there was no need to apologize anymore. He had already said he was sorry about 1,000 times.

There was also no need to make promises, if he was going to do something it would just be better to do it than to talk about it. She told him all the things that she wanted from him and he agreed to it. They talked at least three times a week and she visited him twice a month until the day he got released.

By then JB was a whole different person. He no longer cursed when he talked. He learned how to control his anger. He had no hate in his heart anymore, he learned to love everyone the same. He learned how to love Erica the right way.

He got his second chance at life.

He remembered what the old man Trudi told him when they first met... It's never too late.

# CHAPTER 7

——————◆——————

Once JB was released from prison Erica was there to pick him up. He hadn't held or kissed her for two years, when he did it felt like Heaven.

The first thing they did was see JB's mom.

They decided that it would be best to move in with her until they saved up enough money to get a place of their own. It was a good idea because that way someone would always be there to watch her when the nurse was off.

Cynthia didn't mind because she enjoyed the company.

The other reason was so that Erica wouldn't have to hear the constant lectures from her mom about her taking JB back.

JB went back to work for the construction crew and saved everything he could.

It didn't take long before the streets knew that JB was out. However, JB was very careful and made sure he kept a low profile. He did not want to run into Mike or anybody for that matter. He never went to the block, down the block or anywhere near the neighborhood.

In fact, he didn't go anywhere unless he was with Erica being that she was the only one with a car now. Cynthia had a car but hadn't driven it since she had been diagnosed with cancer.

It didn't take long for the couple to save up enough to move but they didn't want to just leave Cynthia on her own, so they stayed an extra month.

Erica and JB were happy, and living like the past never happened.

They went to church every Sunday.

Erica's mother held a grudge for a while but something came over her, and eventually, she forgave JB for all the pain he caused her daughter.

JB liked his new life; things were looking better for him. He and Erica both agreed that even though she wanted a big dream wedding, the reality was that they were not in a position to do that. They both were starting over from scratch.

Erica had a two year head start on her $8.00 an hour income but the part-time hours she was getting was just not enough. It would take at least one more year to save, and there was no way JB was waiting that long again.

Erica already had the ring but JB got down on one knee and proposed a second time. This time when she said yes they went down to the courthouse and Erica became Mrs. Griffin, they were married.

They went on a small romantic three-day honeymoon in Orlando and they were happier than they had been in their entire lives.

Erica had everything she wanted, because all she wanted was to be someone's wife. All the other things were materialistic and she knew if she got them once she could get them again, and this time she had someone to share them with.

For JB being married meant something else, something more - like a certificate of completion. JB felt like he graduated from high school to college, then from college football to the pros.

He didn't feel like an average person anymore.

He didn't know of one person that was married, not one; at least not anyone his age. Everyone who was married was 55 and over so that made him feel more mature, like he was on another level.

All he needed now was kids to make everything complete.

However, he and Erica knew that they weren't ready for a baby just yet. Erica told JB don't worry, when God felt like they were ready he would make it happen. They had no clue about how fast God works. God's readiness is not ours readiness.

Three weeks after the honeymoon Erica became sick at work. She took the rest of the day off and went home to lie down. When she got there Cynthia wasn't home; she had left with the nurse to go to a doctor's appointment (Cynthia saw the doctor twice a week since the surgeons removed the first tumors. According to the physician, the chemo worked better than any other treatment they could have used and agreed that the cancer looked better).

Erica rested for a couple hours until it was time for school. When she left the house something told her to stop by the store for a pregnancy test. She and JB did agree to wait for kids and they were using protection but there was the night of the honeymoon. People say it only takes one time, but they made love three times that night. She thought well what's done is done.

When she got to school she went straight to the bathroom. She had never taken a pregnancy test before but how hard could it be? She opened the box and read the instructions. When she finished she wrapped it up in a paper towel, dropped it in her purse and went to class.

Later on that day when JB got off of work he got a ride with a guy on his crew. Normally he would get on the bus but it was pouring down raining that day.

JB wasn't too thrilled about riding in the car with people, he didn't trust too many folks. He always had that paranoid feeling of something going wrong and there was no way he was going back to prison, for any reason. His coworker seemed cool though. He was a hard worker, and he always talked about his two daughters so JB didn't take him as the kind of guy who would get into trouble.

That still didn't stop JB from asking the man 50 questions before getting into his car: *Do you have a license? Do you have any guns? Do you have any drugs? Are you wanted? Do you have a warrant? If the police pull you over are you going to run? Does anybody want to kill you?*

JB asked him everything he could think of until he felt safe enough to ride. He even wished the rain would stop so he could catch the bus. Judging by the harsh sound of the thunder and the constant lightning strikes that looked like paparazzi was on the other side of the car taking pictures, the storm was just beginning.

JB put on his seatbelt and said "let's go" the guy just laughed and they drove off. The driver stopped by the store on the way and ran in for a six-pack of Budweiser, JB got out to get a 2-Liter of Pepsi to go with the pizzas they were having for dinner, and yep it was movie night again.

When the two came out of the store there was a man standing on the side of the ice machine. He asked JB, who had his back turned at the time, "excuse me sir could you spare a little bit of change, I'm trying to get something to eat."

When JB turned around he couldn't believe what he was seeing. Standing directly in front of him was Chris. It didn't take him three full seconds to see that Chris was homeless and doing bad, another half second to guess what it was that led him to that point, the drugs. "Chris man what are you doing up here looking like this man?"

"JB that you? Man I'm chilling, trying to get out of this rain. I heard you got out. You looking good too? Let me hold something JB."

"Man... Chris what happened to you bro? How you got like this? I told you to leave that powder alone."

"Man I messed up JB"

"Now look at you"

"I know man, don't do me like that JB help me man."

"Do you like what? You did this to yourself dawg. I don't understand why though. I hate to see you like this bro."

"They got me, they got me good I can't shake it."

"Who got you? What you talking about?"

"Mike them."

"Mike what?"

"Mike and his boys got everybody. They've been running down on a lot of people man. He got me in the bathroom man. I'm just a dead man walking JB."

"Who got you, Mike?"

"No Red … the one that set your house on fire."

"What!" "Yeah they been getting people, you better be careful. He shot me with a needle man, he gave me Aids and Heroine, now I can't shake it. I'm all messed up, Mike done went crazy, and he done took over everything."

JB's coworker blew the horn.

JB said, "Chris, I got ago man, hey I'll give you my number. Call me. Man, I wanna help you, bro."

"Okay… JB let me get five dollars."

JB wrote down his number and gave Chris twenty bucks. JB told Chris again, "Call me man don't forget. Call me in twenty minutes I'll be home."

"Okay JB I got you I won't forget."

JB got back in the car, he couldn't believe what he had just heard. He heard Lil' stories here and there about how Mike had become ruthless, but never imagined that. He knew there was no way he could get in trouble again but if he could get away with it, at that moment JB would've killed Mike with his bare hands, and Red too.

He was so glad that he got away when he did.

He sat on the passenger side quietly thanking God for everything he had done in his life.

When he got home he waited a couple minutes to see if Chris would call but he never did. He thought maybe it was his fault; he had a feeling that Chris took that money straight to the block and got high with it. He felt horrible, and his mother saw it all over his face.

She sat down next to him and they talked about it.

She shared stories with him about friends who had turned to drugs. She reminded him that everyone's story is different. God has a different plan for us all. Her encouragement made JB appreciate life a little more that day.

When his wife walked through the door he looked to at her and thanked God that things were better. He told Erica about his run-in with Chris and about Mike and Red, she just shook her head. She said that she was very proud of him for getting out when he did. They both talked about how sometimes God removes you from a particular place for a reason; we think all is falling apart, but the pieces are all falling together. When the good Lord closes one door, he opens another.

JB went to prison but if he hadn't he probably would be dead or like Chris.

Cynthia chimed in "See baby that's how God works. He sent you away for two years to become a better person. Now you home and you're back with Erica and you two are married. You didn't want to separate but if you would have stayed on the streets you two would have probably ended up losing each other forever."

JB agreed, "Yeah that's crazy how God works. He works in mysterious ways."

Cynthia responded, "Amen now let's eat."

JB asked Erica, "Baby, what movie are we watching tonight?"

Erica responded, "Oh I picked out a good one, go put it in."

JB got up to put on the DVD when he opened the box the pregnancy test fell out. He didn't even look at it he already knew what it meant.

Cynthia screamed...

Erica laughing said, "Gotcha, Ha-ha I got you."

Cynthia asked, "I'm going to have a grandbaby? Yes thank you Jesus."

JB was speechless, he ran over and hugged his wife and said, "It's on now. Let me feel that stomach baby."

Erica replied, "There ain't nothing to feel yet Jonathan. I don't think is going to happen that fast."

"How did you find out? When did you know?"

"I found out today after school, I got sick at work and left. I came here to lie down then I went to the store. When I got to school I took the test, but I didn't looked at it until after class. I was so happy."

JB responded, "I'm glad too."

JB's mom replied, "I'm happy too."

Erica stated, "Well I know we said that we was going to wait but it's happening now so there's nothing we can do about it. I still have to go to the doctor and see exactly how far along I am. I haven't told my mom yet either, I wanted you to be the first one to know baby. If everything goes right you're going to be a daddy."

JB responded, "No we are going to be parents, and good ones too."

Cynthia gathered the two of them in a circle and she prayed: *Dear Lord we come to you in the mighty name of Jesus. We thank you for this baby, for this beautiful life that you have blessed this loving couple with today. We ask that you go through this pregnancy with Erica and see that everything goes right from now on to the time she delivers. Whether it be a little girl a little boy or both we ask that it be healthy. Father God bless this marriage and take it to another level. May this baby bring these two closer than they ever thought they could be. You made this Lord and we know that you do not mess up or make mistakes.*

*So again we thank you for this new life. We give you all the praise, we give you all the glory forever and ever in Jesus name we pray Amen.*

And just as Cynthia had prayed, instantly a spirit of love rushed through the house. Erica and JB sat and watched movies and held each other close for the rest of the night. They didn't even go to the bedroom, they fell asleep right there on the couch.

* * *

Saturday morning JB cooked breakfast for everyone. He and Erica both had the day off, so after breakfast they went apartment hunting. They came to the conclusion that with the baby, they would definitely need to be on their own.

Cynthia could handle JB and Erica living with her but a crying baby might be a bit much for Cynthia.

JB started daydreaming about how it would be to be a father. He was in a daze and didn't hear Erica ask him a question.

"Baby are you ignore me?"

"Huh? Oh no baby, never. I was just thinking about some things. What did you say?"

"What part of the city do you want to stay on, Southside or Northside?"

JB replied, "As far away from the hood as possible."

"Remember honey we still have to get back and forth to work."

"Oh yeah I forgot about that. But by the time we move, I should have a car. I'm thinking about buying

**211**

a cheap car, something like $1200-$1500. It ain't gotta be nothing fancy. I just don't want our son (he looked at her) or daughter growing up in the hood. I don't want them going through all the things I had to go through. It's so easy to get caught up out here.

When I used to be on the block I saw how bad the kids were, and all they were doing was trying to be like us. Kids do what they see others doing. I want my children to see *good* and do *good*."

"Kids? Okay you jumping the gun mister, let's get this one out of the stomach first and see how that goes before we mention more."

"Oh you better get ready girl, you gonna be spitting them out like sunflower seeds."

They both laughed

Then Erica asked, "Why don't you help kids baby?"

"What you mean?"

Erica said, "Start something for the youth. Show them that selling dope and hanging on the block ain't the way to live. I bet you can do it, people listened to you before they'll listen to you again. I think you should seriously think about it baby, it'll be sexy."

"Sexy! What!"

'Yes, a hard working positive man like you, out here helping kids be something in life. That turns me on so I know I will have to fight their mothers off you."

JB laughed and said, "You crazy."

"I'm serious, the women better stay away from my husband."

"I know you serious that's why I love you."

Erica responded, "I love you too."

"Starbucks."

Erica said, "Oh boy I haven't heard the name in forever... speaking of that name baby, when was the last time you heard from Chris?"

"I didn't, he never called me, and I only saw him that one time."

"Do you think he's alright?"

"I don't know, he living on the street so it ain't like I can go to his house."

Erica replied, "I remember that he was so funny, always cracking jokes."

"Yeah that's my boy, class clown ever since elementary school. That day I saw him though, he was a whole different person. He was skinny, his face was all sunk in and stuff."

"Baby, that's why I thank God that you did what you said you was going to do and got out. I loved you before but I love the man you have become even more, and I'm glad to be your wife."

"Aww my baby sound like a white girl."

Erica punched him in the shoulder. Erica said, "Shut up... would you rather me sound like a ghetto queen?"

"See you almost made me curse. Naw big head I like you just like that."

They drove around looking for apartments. They went online and compared different prices. It took a while but eventually they found the perfect little two bedroom.

Cynthia was happy for them but also sad because she had gotten used to them being around. She had been living on her own for almost eight years since her husband was killed in a car crash. He was JB's sister's father.

She dated guys periodically but no one ever lived there with her after him. She forgot how it felt to have someone else in the house with her, and she was going to miss them.

Two weeks later JB and Erica packed up all their things and moved out. JB found an inexpensive car just like he said he would, something that could get him back and forth to work.

Other than that, he and Erica were inseparable.

They were always together, when you saw one you saw the other, they were best friends. Erica's mom saw how close the two were and how much her daughter had grown up and thanked JB for being a man and loving her daughter. They started to become a little closer themselves, she even called him son, and told him she loved him.

JB's mom, Cynthia felt a lot of love as well; it seemed like all that love gave her strength. She had been seeing the doctor like always and he told her that the cancer was looking good.

That was good news for her because although she felt like she was putting up a tough fight, in the back of her mind she had a feeling that her days were so slowly counting down. She heard stories of people surviving cancer but all the ones she knew personally didn't. Did she have faith and believe that God will heal her?

Of course but was she still nervous?

Yes. And it still hurt every time she looked in the mirror. She had completely lost all of our hair and her weight had dropped down 36 pounds. She always wore her wig and kept a smile on her face so if you didn't know her you would never guess that she was going through anything at all.

Friends that did know of her situation always kept Cynthia in their prayers. Cynthia had a relationship with God but because of a personal experience dealing with false prophets and fake pastors she stayed away from church. She felt more comfortable studying at home but after seeing the change in her son she let the past be the past and decided she would go back to church.

A few days later Cynthia returned to the doctor's office. However, she didn't expect to hear what she heard on this particular visit.

The cancer was gone, there was no trace of it anywhere, like it had never been there.

She was shocked and the thing that surprised her is that the doctor was just as shocked as she was. He heard of such things like that happening before but never saw it for himself in all the 23 years of his career.

When she left the doctor's office she couldn't wait to call someone and tell them the good news. First, she called her sister Janice, then she called her daughter in Texas.

She wanted to tell JB last, he was her baby boy, they were close. When she called him, he thought something was wrong because she never called him, he always call her first.

"Momma what's wrong you alright?"

Cynthia crying and smiling at the same time said, "Its gone baby... the good Lord took it away."

"What mom, what's gone the cancer?"

"Yes Jonathan! The doctor said he couldn't find any trace of it like it was never there. Hallelujah thank you Jesus I'm so happy."

"Me too I can't believe it."

Erica heard JB yelling so she came running. "What happened baby?"

"My momma cancer is gone, the doctor couldn't find it. She beat it."

"Oh my God! That's so good. Let me talk to her." Erica got on the phone. "Hey mama I'm so happy for you. Won't he do it?"

"Yes He will baby. I can't tell you how I feel right now."

Erica said, "I know mama... you don't have to because I can bet you jumping through the ceiling right now."

JB chimed in, "Hey I wanna hear, put it on speaker phone."

The three of them talked and laughed back and forth about how good God is for at least a half hour.

The Holy Spirit was all over the place that day; He was moving. Like never before, JB knew God was real as the ground he was standing on. He couldn't believe it took him as long as it did to realize that life was so much better when you live it for God.

Everything was falling into place.

Everything he lost he had gained it back. He had his girl back, he had a place to live, he had a car, a legit job, he was earning legal money, his mother was back healthy and now he was going to be a father.

If life didn't get better than that, he wouldn't care at all, it was good enough how it was.

He gave God all of the Glory.

# CHAPTER 8

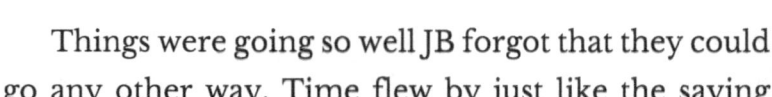

Things were going so well JB forgot that they could go any other way. Time flew by just like the saying goes, when you're having fun.

Before JB knew it Erica was 6 months pregnant, with a boy, and now showing. They were happy but couldn't seem to come up with a name. Erica wanted a junior but JB never liked his name so Jonathan was out of the question.

He always got a kick out of seeing the waves in Erica's stomach as the baby turned, but her stomach wasn't the only thing that was changing.

Things were about turn real bad real quick.

One day while Erica was on the way home from school a car pulled out in front of her. She was able to avoid the accident; however, hitting the brakes as hard as she did it caused her to fly forward. The seatbelt jerked against her stomach so tight it sent a numbing type feeling all through her body. She was so scared she didn't go home, she drove straight to the hospital.

Immediately she called JB and he rushed down there to meet her.

After getting an ultrasound and other tests the doctors said that the baby's heart was still beating and there was no damage. Erica walked away with a minor bruise as a result of the seatbelt. They were lucky that time, but they both knew that it could have been much worse.

They thanked God for keeping the little one safe.

From that day forward Erica paid extra close attention when she drove on the road and was cautious about everything.

Erica and Jonathan (JB) always did the right things and attempted to live a godly life, yet no matter what they did, the devil managed to sneak in. He went at JB Hard, trying all kinds of tricks and schemes. Despite satan's devices Erica and Jonathan continued to pray and praise God together.

JB and Erica never argued before the pregnancy, but lately they found themselves disagreeing almost every day. Erica would complain about every little thing and JB would get tired of hearing it. Erica might ask JB a question and would not like the answer he gave back. She would nag and nag until JB would just get up and walk out of the house. This went on so much that JB started to perform poorly at work.

His concentration was gone and he even began to get into arguments with a few of his coworkers.

One Monday morning when the crew got to the jobsite the foreman discovered that the tool shed had been broken into. An expensive jackhammer and a few other tools were missing. He questioned JB about the theft because he had been acting strange the past couple of weeks.

The company called the police and they came out to take fingerprints and began a small investigation. The owner told JB that if he was found guilty of any involvement in the crime that he would not only be fired but charges would be brought against him.

JB told his Foreman and the owner that he had been going through a tough time at home with his wife that's why his work performance might have dropped, but in no way was he a thief.

At lunchtime, JB called his wife just as he did every day but the night before Erika forgot to put her phone on the charger so it was dead. When she didn't answer JB thought she was still mad and ignoring him.

That is what the devil wanted him to believe.

At the end of the day when work was over JB had so many things on his mind he stopped by the store to get something to drink. He sat in the car thinking long and hard about everything. About how far he had come, and how fast he lost everything the last time he took a drink.

Leaving the bottle unopened, he threw it in the trash and went home.

When Erica got home from school he had flowers sitting on the table. They were the same kind of flowers he gave her on their first date at the beach. He sat her down and held her hand. He told her how terrible he had been feeling the past couple of weeks and that he wanted things to go back the way they were before.

They sat and talked and spilled out their hearts to one another and put it all behind them and shared their love with one another passionately that night.

Just when things seemed to be going back to normal something else happened, something far greater than disagreeing and arguments.

JB got word of a rumor that was spreading fast in the city and his name was right in the middle of it. He found out that for the last year and a half the FBI was doing an investigation on Michael Douglas Wilson... yep his childhood friend Mike.

Mike was being investigated for not only trafficking and distribution of drugs but also for a string of kidnappings and murders throughout St. Petersburg and nearby cities including Miami, Ocala, Orlando and Daytona.

JB was surprised but not shocked.

He saw how fast Mike's drug career had grown in just a short time before he went to prison. He was shocked at how in only 2 years Mike became one of the biggest and most feared drug dealers in Florida. He knew that if Mike would come after his best friend to get to the top, he would run over anybody in his way to stay there.

The thing that surprised him, though, was how his name ended up in the mix.

He knew that he had done nothing wrong, he also knew that the police in his city arrest first and ask questions later. There was no way he was going back to prison, no way. He called around to see if there was any truth to the rumor but no one would give him any information.

It didn't matter because before he knew it the information came to him.

Cynthia told JB about the one day she saw a suspicious looking car parked in the alley behind her house. She said she didn't see anyone inside but she just thought it was odd.

Mr. Ru from across the street also mentioned that he saw two men walking from behind her house but his eyesight isn't so good so he couldn't tell if it was JB or not.

JB wondered why someone was behind his mother's house. Could it be someone trying to break in? Could it be someone waiting for him to show up so they could rob him? He really didn't know what to think. He told Mr. Ru that it wasn't him so keep a look out, and if he saw them again to call the police.

Mr. Ru was old so he didn't have much to do anyways, he enjoyed stalking out Cynthia's house every day, but he never did see the two men return.

Cynthia never saw that suspicious car again either.

JB started to get that paranoid feeling all over again. He paid close attention to his surroundings.

While at work one day he noticed a car parked alongside the road off at a distance. The car hadn't moved in 4 hours. No one got in and he saw no one get out.

A few of his coworkers noticed the same thing.

On his lunch break, JB walked down the street to the car and saw two men sitting inside. He knocked on the window and just as he expected, when the window came down it was two agents.

"Hello Mr. Griffin how are you?"

"Why are you watching me, man? I ain't did nothing..."

"Well if you haven't done anything then you shculdn't have anything to worry about should you? Since you are here though let's have a little talk."

"Man... I swear I don't know nothing. I've been working ever since I got out of prison. I'm married and I got a baby on the way. I don't do nothing, I don't get in trouble."

"So you're trying to tell us that you're not partners with Michael Wilson? We know how close you two are. Come on Jonathan, that's your best friend, you grew up together right?"

"Naw, I mean yeah we grew up together and was best friends but I ain't seen him since I went to prison, and I ain't trying to see him."

"We know you think you're smart Jonathan but we're smarter. It is just a matter of time, we're going to get you and when we do this time you're not getting out, we'll be in touch."

The agent rolled up the window and drove off.

JB was scared out of his mind. He didn't know what was going on. Going back to prison and never getting out, he almost had a heart attack.

He prayed right there in the street: *Lord please fix this, make it quick God. You know I'm innocent. The devil is a liar, he's trying to take your child father, don't let him.*

He started thinking, *how did my name get in the middle of all of this madness?* But when you're best friends with one of the most dangerous criminals in Florida anything's possible.

He went back to work and thought about it. He thought about it so much that he came up with a plan. He was going to do a little investigation of his own. After work he went to BestBuy and bought a cheap video surveillance camera system.

He hooked it up outside of his mom's house.

He set up 4 cameras around the house. One under the mailbox facing the house, the 2nd one in a tree capturing the side of the house where Mr. Ru saw the two guys walking. The 3rd one on top of a shed in the back of the house to look down the alley, and the 4th one he put on top of the house facing the street to see any and everyone who drove by or walked up to the door.

A few weeks later the FBI tracked down and arrested Red, the same guy who burned down JB's house and stuck Chris with the needle at the bar. Red thought he would be okay by hiding out at his girlfriend's house in Lakeland which was an hour from St. Petersburg where the shooting took place.

Local authorities in Lakeland say a hotel owner reported suspicious activity. When the police went to check it out Red took off on foot to a nearby gas station, where he snatched a lady out of her car and managed to lose police through the neighborhood.

They caught him about twenty minutes later speeding down I-4. Once the authorities had him in custody they hit him with all types of questions.

"What are you doing in Lakeland?" "Who are you working for?" "Where is Michael Wilson?"

The police handed Red over to the FBI who told him that they knew all about the murders and kidnappings. They even knew about the fire from the statement Erica gave two years before.

"Yes sir Red, we've been looking for you for a long time. "You're pretty good at running, but not good enough."

"I want a lawyer."

"Yeah I'm pretty sure you do; but here's the thing - A lawyer can't help you son, you're finished."

They told Red that they would be willing to offer a deal. Instead of asking for the death penalty they would be easy on him and just give him life. He would have to give up some names first, and the name they wanted most was Michael Wilson.

Red refused to talk, but he did give up one name, JB.

He denied even knowing who Michael was, he told the agents that JB was his boss. That JB was the one supplying him and sending him on missions since he came home from prison.

The FBI had been watching JB close since he came back, so they didn't buy that story for one second. However, they did know that JB was once a big name in the drug game so chances are he could've had a hand in it, but he wasn't the boss.

JB knew that it was a matter of time before police came after him with more questions, so he warned Erica ahead of time.

"Baby the FBI is looking for Mike, and for some unknown reason he decided to put my name in the mix."

"What! Why would he do that?"

"Beats me, baby, nobody wants to go to jail, not even him so right about now he'll do anything to get out of it. He ain't gonna get away this time though, they are on him too heavy. It's the FBI, when they come, 9 times out of 10 they already got you.

I just gotta get my name out of it.

Now you know I've been with you every day since I came home so ain't no way I had anything to do with this. You do know that right baby?"

"Yes baby, I know but I can't deal with you going back."

"Listen, I ain't going nowhere, the devil trying to take what we have but he is a liar. He ain't got no power you know that. We gone trust God and let him work this thing out okay Erica?"

"Okay."

The FBI came quick. Two hours later they were knocking on his door.

"Hello Erica is your husband home? We would like to have a word with him."

"He's not going to jail, is he?"

"As of right now no; we just need to ask him some questions is he in there?"

"Yeah, I'm right here," JB was in the back room and came out. "What's up?"

"Hey Jonathan how you doing tonight?"

"I'm fine what's up?"

"I'm gonna need you to come down to the station and answer some questions."

They took JB down to the station and Erica followed. They asked JB a lot of questions. Things like "Did he know where Mike might be hiding out?" "How well did he know Red?" "Was he the supplier?" 'Were he and Mike partners?"

Of course, JB said no to all the questions.

They kept him there for 2 ½ hours until they gathered up as much information as they could. They even tried to trick JB by telling him that they had Mike in the other room saying that he was the leader and that unless he came clean he would spend the rest of his life in prison.

JB had no money for lawyer, all he had was God.

He cooperated and let the agents do their job, but there was nothing more they could do, without any evidence they would have to let JB walk free.

That's when Red dropped the bomb. He said, "*Okay, okay* I'll tell you where the stash house at." Red gave the FBI and address and told them exactly where to look.

The address was Cynthia's house.

Just when they were about to let JB free they sat him back down. The agents left the room. Fifteen minutes later they came back in.

JB asked, "Man was sup when ya'll gone let me go? I know ya'll ain't got nothing on me."

The agent responded, "Whoa Mr. speedy don't get cocky just yet. We just received information that your mother's house is actually the stash house, you care to tell us about that?"

"What? My momma house ain't no stash house."

"I have a couple field officers headed over there right now to check it out."

"Yeah you go check it out because it ain't no stash house over there." That's when JB thought about the suspicious car and the two men. Somebody was trying to set him up.

"Hey! Naw man they want to set me up. Hey, officer, I'm telling you I know somebody wants to set me up. My momma said she saw a car parked and the neighbor across the street said two dudes were walking in my momma yard."

When the field officers got there they asked Cynthia if they could search the house. They brought in the dogs but there was nothing inside. The dogs led them to the back of the house where they found thirty-five kilos of cocaine and over $100,000 in cash.

When the officers called it back into the station, the agents put JB in cuffs.

Back at the house officers were just about to arrest Cynthia also when an officer came out of the house and said, "Sir you might want to take a look at this."

The police officer played the video from the cameras. He hit rewind and the tape showed three men pulling up in a blue car and opening the trunk. They stashed the drugs and money under the porch and drove away. They brought the video back to the station and gave it to the analyst for a closer review.

It only took the investigators two minutes to see that the guys who placed the drugs under the house were the same guys who were on camera at the hotel with Red earlier that day.

JB was right, after all, he had been set up, and the FBI apologized to JB and let him go.

They still had Red though, and he wasn't going anywhere. They were now on the lookout for a blue Dodge charger and the three guys. After all that they still were not even one step closer to finding Mike.

On the way home JB looked at Erica and said, "I bet you were getting ready to leave me again wasn't you?"

"Nope, I knew you wasn't going anywhere."

"How you knew that?"

"That's what I prayed for when I was following ya'll and God told me not to worry, so I didn't."

"That's my baby, I love you."

"I love you too."

"Now let's go to my momma's house and see if she's alright."

"Yes I know she probably was as scared as I was, let me call her right now."

"*Hello.*"

"Hey Ma its Erica, you alright?"

*"Child yes I'm just over here across the street laughing with Mr. Ru and his wife. I wish I would've known I had $100,000 sitting under my house; I tell you what, it would've been gone."*

Erica in shock asked, "$100,000 baby why you ain't say it was $100,000?"

JB replied, "I ain't know, they ain't tell me nothing. I wish I would've knew, but I'm glad I didn't."

"Yeah you right because I can't take no more of this. I hope they hurry up and do catch Mike because he's trying to take my husband down with him."

*"No he ain't taking nobody down with him, that's what he get. I'm glad my son finally came to his senses and woke up."*

"Me too Ma."

*"Baby, God always wins over evil every time. I know the devil mad because his plan didn't work. The Bible says that God will make your enemies our footstool."*

"I know that's right, we was about to come over there and check on you, you gonna be alright by yourself tonight?"

*"Yes ya'll go home, I'm gone sit on my couch and watch TV and watch these cameras to see if anybody gonna put some more money up under my house you understand me?"*

"I hear you Ma you do that."

JB chimed in saying, "Tell her I said I love her."

"Ma Jonathan said he loves you."

*"Tell him I love him too, and I love you too baby. I love all three of you. Speaking of the baby, don't tell me you still haven't come up with a name for my grandson yet."*

"Nope but that's what we gone go home and do right now."

JB being funny said, "Go home and do what? The nasty?"

Erica replied, "No boy! Ha-ha come up with a name for the baby."

JB chuckled and said, "Oh."

"We'll talk to you later Ma good night."

*"Good night ya'll."*

"Hey baby, JB asked Erica, what you think about Mercy?"

"What you mean?"

"For the baby's name; I don't know anybody named Mercy."

"Me either, if that's what you want then I guess. It sounds kind of funny."

"That's because you ain't said it 100 times yet baby. You'll get used to it."

"Dang Jonathan look, what done happened up there?"

There were police, lights and paramedics about a mile down the road from where they were. JB couldn't drive close enough to see what happened because the road was blocked.

"Just turn right here and go down to central."

"Alright hold on let me ask this lil dude what happened."

There were two teenage boys riding bikes down the sidewalk, JB stopped them to ask what happened. "Hey ya'll know what happened up there"

"Naw they just found a man on the side of the store dead."

Erica stated, "Oh wow! That's crazy."

JB replied, "Yeah that is, let's hurry up and get home baby." JB turned to face the kid and said, "alright lil man ya'll be safe out here."

Erica said to JB, "See baby its little boys just like that who you could be teaching. They look like they be getting in trouble."

JB responded, "Look at you judging people's kids."

"I'm just saying baby, I bet you won't leave your car running around them."

JB just smiled and shook his head.

"Yeah you know I'm right. I really think you should do that. You actually could make a lot of money doing it. So you won't have to be busting your back at that construction job coming home all dirty and stank."

"Oh I be stank?"

"Yeah you be stankin."

JB put his arm pit in Erica's face, laughed hysterically and then said, "I bet you love my stinkiness."

Erica replied, "Ewe no I don't."

The two of them went home and relaxed for the rest of the night. JB warmed some left overs in the microwave, they took a shower together, and they laid down on the bed. They talked while JB massaged his wife's feet. After that they listened to TD Jakes until they fell asleep.

* * *

Erica woke up at five am and turned on the news like she did every morning; she started getting ready for work (news reporter).

*At approximately 8:45 PM last night police received a report of a dead body by the* **Stop and Shop Food Store** *on 9th Ave., North. Authorities say Chris Stevenson overdosed on heroin.*

Erica stared at the screen and the sound faded into the distance. She ran into the room to wake up JB. "Baby, baby that was Chris last night, he's dead."

Groggy, JB responded, "Oh my God Chris is dead?"

"Yes. Chris died last night of a heroin overdose. Remember when we saw all those paramedics and fire trucks?"

"Yeah ...yeah that was Chris?"

"Yes baby he's gone, he overdosed, I'm so sorry. I had to wake you up and let you know but I have to finish getting ready for work."

She saw the blank look on his face.

'Are you sure you're going to be okay?"

'Yeah I just can't believe it."

He went to the living room to see for himself but the news had already gone off. Erica felt sorry for him because she knew he'd never lost anyone close to him before except his grandmother when he was 5, his grandfather at age 8 and his Auntie Mary when he was 15; however, neither of those deaths affected him.

However waking up to hear about his friend Chris' death tore him apart.

He thought about that rainy day at the store. How he wished that his friend could have been stronger.

He prayed for him but never actually talked to him about giving his life to Christ. He didn't like how he last saw Chris, all he could think about was him suffering. Deep down inside he knew that it was partly his fault.

A week and a half later at Chris's funeral JB said a small speech:

*"Chris was my friend. A brother from another mother. Chris was a good dude. There was nothing bad about him, except a few of his jokes. They were horrible. No I take that back sometimes he was funny, and thoughtful. He would give*

*you the shirt off his back if you needed it. Then turn around and tell you how funny you looked in it.*

*That was him, the comedian.*

*We always had each other's back. He even wrestled this dude that had a gun once. Yeah he was crazy too, but sometimes you have to be a little crazy to be a hero. If it wasn't for him I might be dead and he'd be the one up here speaking. I just want to tell my friend that I'm sorry for not kidnapping him that day in the rain and taking him to rehab. But now he doesn't need rehab because he got something better.*

*He got GOD.*

*He's probably up there right now cracking jokes with the Angels. Saying look Jesus, look at that tight suit JB got on, I bet $100 Starbucks picked it out for him. Look like she got it from her baby cousin Harry.*

*I love you Chris rest in peace."*

After that speech the whole church was crying.

After the funeral JB made up his mind to take Erica's advice. He turned to Erica and said, "Baby I think you was right as a matter of fact I know you was right."

"Right about what?"

"I need to help people, I could've helped Chris. I'm going to start that business, I'm going to show these kids out here that there is another way to live. Tell them about God and how we have to always stay focused on doing the right thing because the devil never stops coming."

Erica responded, "Right, when you block him from the front he comes from the back. When you turn around, he hits you from the side. When you look over he comes from the top and the bottom at the same time."

JB commented, "Exactly! We have to get covered. The streets ain't nothing but a dead-end road. Sometimes we are so hardheaded. We see the road closed and still try to figure out a way to squeeze through, and always end up getting stuck. GOD puts up the detour signs for a reason. That's what I'm going to name it baby."

"You're going name it detour?"

"Yep. The *Detour Foundation*, to help kids, teens and young adults; and stop them from going down that dead-end road."

And that's what JB set out to do …

# CHAPTER 9

──────⟨◇⟩──────

JB made up his mind that it was time to go to the next level. He made it as a drug dealer, he went to prison twice, and then he got off the streets and became a Christian. Now he was going to start a foundation that would help others do the same.

He wanted to catch them before they start and set them on the right track. He was onto something; he finally found his calling.

*Could this be what God had in store for him the whole time? Was his whole life designed for this very moment right here?*

It had to be, and there was no way he went through all he had been through just to become a construction worker living in a two bedroom apartment.

He felt like he had a bigger purpose.

He always had the kind of attitude like he was too good for certain things, maybe he was, too good for the streets. He was excited about starting the business, but he didn't know the first thing about how to do it. He was aware that his smart wife could help, but she had enough going on already with her work, school and being pregnant.

Plus he thought it was already her idea, what kind of man would he be if she came up with the idea and did it for him? It should be the other way around; he should be guiding her. He was working, but he would need to work a little bit harder.

He called up the pastor and told him about his plan to create a youth ministry.

Even though the church already had a youth ministry he knew from personal experience how difficult it was to bring kids from the neighborhood into the church; therefore, his plan was to bring the church into the neighborhoods.

This opened JB's eyes to a whole new world he never even dreamed of. He could become somebody famous; maybe he would be pastor of a church

245

someday. No he didn't want to be a pastor that was pushing it. He figured he'd have to be too perfect for that, one or two mess ups and God would strike him with lightning.

Who knows? Maybe one day he could run for City Council or maybe even become the Mayor. He thought, *Yeah Mayor Griffin ex-drug dealer cleaning up the streets of St. Petersburg.*

Okay he was getting too far ahead of himself; it would take at least another ten to fifteen years to pull that off. He needed to get started on a much smaller scale.

That's when he thought about it, he didn't even have any experience in what it was he was trying to do. That was like a rookie basketball player coming out of college trying to skip playing and become head coach of a pro team.

He had to get experience so that's what he did, he found the perfect person to practice on.

A young white boy who lived right next door.

He had to be about eighteen or nineteen. A spoiled little brat living off his mom and dad's money. A skateboard freak who did nothing but party, party, and party and when he wasn't partying, he slept off his hangovers from partying. He figured he could mentor the kid just like Mr. Trudi mentored him in prison. It was a good idea but he would never get a chance to do it.

The landlord kicked the kid out two days later for too many noise complaints. JB tried talking to the guys at his job but he didn't get very far at all. He ran right into a brick wall, no one wanted to listen to him preach about God or changing the way they were living.

Getting to the heart was harder than one man single-handedly taken over the White House; he wouldn't get past the front gate.

One thing about it, if a person doesn't want to receive it you can't force it on them.

He never thought that talking to people about Jesus would be so tough. He had no problem listening to Mr. Trudi talk about salvation, he even wanted to hear.

Okay so everybody wasn't like him. He wasn't giving up though, he was going to find somebody, but who? It would have to be someone who wasn't just going to up and disappear in two days.

That's when he thought about *Can Man*.

*Can Man* was an older guy who came down the alley every day digging through the dumpster collecting aluminum cans. He didn't know if he was homeless or not but he sure acted like it. He may have changed clothes twice every two weeks, and never went anywhere without that shopping cart.

JB didn't know where he hung out, slept or ate.

The only time he saw *Can Man* was either in the alley or walking down the street here and there, but he did see him every day so that would give him plenty of time to talk to him.

Usually, JB slept in an extra hour after his lovely wife left for work, but this Tuesday JB decided to stay up.

After Erica left JB went into the closet and picked out a pair of old shoes, a hat he had not worn in months, two pair of jeans, three T-shirts and a jacket. He got cleaned up, ate a bowl of cereal then went out back to wait for Can Man to pass through.

It was just after 7:00 am, JB waited and several minutes had passed but Can Man hadn't shown up. JB started to think he wasn't going to.

Thirty minutes had passed and still no Can Man.

He didn't want to be late for work but he waited five more minutes anyway. Then *Can Man* came pushing that loud squeaky cart down the alley.

JB stopped him and started talking to him.

"Hey wassup man? Good morning. I see you out here getting these early morning cans."

"Yeah I gotta grab them before the garbage trucks come."

"Yeah... that's a good idea. You make any money off all them bags you be having?"

"Not a lot maybe 4 or 5 dollars... sometimes I might find other things like the radio or something."

"Hmmm ... listen I got something better. I got a bag of clothes right here for you. Just two outfits a jacket and a pair of shoes."

"Aww man thank you God bless you."

"Well, yeah you welcome but don't thank me, thank GOD." God has blessed me so it's only right that I bless someone else you know?

Check this out, I gotta get to work like right now but where you gonna be at later? I want you to stop by and knock on this door, I really want talk to you. I would like to help you if I can. JB asked, "Can you get here around 6:00 pm or 6:30 pm?"

Can Man responded, "I eat dinner at the shelter at six but I can come after that. What do you want to talk to me about?"

"Oh... just life man, get to know you a little bit, like I said maybe I can help you out. There definitely ain't no future in selling cans feel me. I gotta go though, I hope those clothes can fit you, come back tonight."

JB left for work. Just that one small good deed was enough to make him feel good inside. When JB got to work his foreman pulled him to the side for a talk.

"Hey JB... you got a second? Come over here right quick let me speak to you."

"Sure...what's going on?"

"Well... first off I want to apologize to you for that accident that happened a couple weeks ago. The police did their investigation, and they found out who broke into the tool shed, so I'm sorry for that."

JB responded, "See... I tried to tell you I ain't have nothing to do with that. Ya'll should have cameras up anyway."

"Yeah we're putting some up, we should have them sometime this week but again I'm sorry."

His boss continued ...

"Now another thing I want to talk to you about is your performance. I noticed that something had been bothering you these past few weeks, actually everyone could tell. But I see you still coming here on time every day and busting your butt for me and I appreciate it. You don't come high or smelling like a brewery and like I said you do work. I haven't had any problems out of you since you came back. For that I've decided to give you a dollar raise."

"Wow thank you."

"No problem you earned it but I just expect to see that same hustle out of you still, deal?"

"Aww man deal, you ain't gotta worry about me. I'm still gone be the same person and do the same thing I been doing."

"That's what I like to hear, now go clock in and get to work."

He patted JB on the back. JB had a smile on his face.

Now he thought, *was the raise given because I really have been busting my tail, or was the foreman just embarrassed by sort of blaming me for the tools coming up missing? It could've been because I gave those clothes to Can Man.* Then he thought to himself, *"If it was because of that then God sure works fast."*

It didn't matter, whatever the reason he was glad to have it.

Later on that day when he got home he started thinking about Chris. Thinking about Chris got him thinking about all his friends and how none of them were around anymore.

Every last one of them ended up dead or was in some kind of trouble, he was the only one that made it out.

*Was it their fault for not following him to the new life of Christianity or was his fault for not inviting them?*

That's what he couldn't figure out.

For a second he thought it would be fun for all of them to hang out at some of the church picnics, kind of how they use to do on the block, but who was he kidding? Some things were just meant to end. Old life, old friends ... yeah that made sense.

What didn't make sense though, was that he didn't have new friends to go with his new life.

Sure some of the guys at the church were cool but it wasn't the same. That close bond just wasn't there, they were only what he considered 'Sunday morning service, Wednesday night Bible study and every now and again church event friends.'

The guys at the job he didn't consider as friends either, they were just co-workers. Work, work, work ... with a few laughs here and there – then more work.

He only had two real friends, his wife and God... he didn't even have a dog. He sat there on the couch thanking God over and over.

JB had a lot on his mind.

All his goals, short term goals, long term goals and all his big dreams; yet one thing he never thought to consider was what might be on GOD's mind.

His Mom was proud of him and she often gave advice on how he should live. Erica had a good idea about what he could do with his life also. He liked their ideas so much it got him thinking even deeper about things he could do, but he forgot to ask the most important person.

So down on his knees he went ...

*"In Jesus name, I pray. Lord I know I am a sinner, in my life I did a lot of bad things. I don't deserve to be here. I was sinking fast but your grace, mercy and unconditional love has placed my feet on solid ground. You gave me yet another chance and I thank you Lord, I praise you Lord.*

*Before I was trying to control my life but now I'm asking you to take over. Lord show me what it is you want me to do. I'm only human, my ideas are only ideas but your plans are what will be.*

*Lord I rather not make my life any harder than it has to be so please show me your way so I can avoid less mistakes as possible. I'm all yours God do with me what you wish, use me, Father God.*

*In Jesus' mighty name I pray Amen!"*

He just sat there on his knees meditating for a while thanking and praising Jesus. He heard a car door slam and the sound of keys.

It was his wife coming home from work.

JB met her at the door with a hug and a kiss... "Hey honey... how was your day?"

"Whew, this baby is kicking my butt, I'm so ready for him to come out so you can have him. Other than that it was alright; nothing to brag on. What about you? I see you haven't took a shower yet, did you work late today?"

"Naw I just been sitting thinking about a lot then I prayed. I just finished right now before I heard your car door close."

"Oh yeah, what were you praying about, can I know, can I be nosey?"

"Just asking God to take over because I'm always thinking about what I want to do. I ain't trying to set a plan, get my hopes up and get disappointed when He do what He wants. So I just basically asked Him to do it and told Him wherever he leads me I am ready to follow.

Oh yeah and guess what baby?"

"What, let me guess? You love me?"

"You know it . . . every second of every minute, but I went to work today, and Jason gave me a dollar raise."

"That's great baby. He probably feels guilty about blaming you for stealing them tools."

"That's what I said too. Oh and I gave *Can Man* some clothes and shoes this morning. He supposed to be coming over here probably about 7:00 pm so I can talk to him. I think I wanna try to help him like I should have helped Chris, God bless the dead."

"Yeah that would be nice if you do that baby, I know he would appreciate it."

"Yeah I know I would if I was in his position."

*Can Man* was in a position alright, he had gotten so drunk he was passed out under the Interstate five blocks away from the shelter. He collected a few dollars from the cans and panhandled a few more dollars until he got up enough for a fifth of Vodka. He never made it back that night to talk to JB.

JB didn't see him the next day either.

Now he was second-guessing, "Was that a sign?" Was God trying to tell him something? Maybe it wasn't meant for him to do what he was trying to do. Maybe God wanted him to do something else, after all, he did pray for God to take control.

That didn't stop him from helping people though.

Every so often he would buy a homeless person McDonald's or something. He might see a woman

256

standing under a roof cover trying to dodge the rain and give her his umbrella. When he and Erica would be in line at the grocery store he would donate to a cancer fund or a local charity.

Small things like that left JB feeling joyful, it was something about giving that gave him power, almost like it seemed to give him life. Erica liked it also, she was so amazed at who her husband had become. She had watched him grow up right in front of her eyes.

When she met him, he was doing work for the devil, but now he was doing God's work.

However, JB didn't call it work; for him it was merely a hobby, something he just enjoyed doing.

Every chance he got, he spoke to someone about the walk with Christ. No long conversations, just a few words here and there ...

Questions like *"Do you know God loves you?" "Jesus is the answer to all your problems." "A little faith takes you a long way." "Smile, it's not over until God says is over." "Every day is a new day."*

He felt like everyone could use a word of encouragement every once in a while. He had some easy days and some hard ones. Many days he got smiles, while other days he got a good cursing out. Some folks listened but had their own opinion; others just didn't want to hear anything at all.

He started typing the quotes on small business card type papers. He began passing them out here and there, or if Erica ran into a store and said she was only going to be in there for five minutes but meant twenty or thirty, he just walked through the parking lot placing them under peoples windshield wipers.

He often saw different people in church telling their testimonies and boy did he have one of his own.

He was just a little on the long-winded side, it would literally take about three Sundays to tell his story. That's when he came out with the idea of writing a book.

A book about his life, but not all of his life – not just his life... okay just a book about life, there you go.

A book about how it's so easy to get so deeply caught up in the wrong that you think it's right. Then when you try to do right it is too late.

All he wanted to do was help people get it right the first time, because that's what Jesus would have done right?

After weeks of research he finally had enough information to start putting together a small business plan for his *Detour Foundation*. He was really excited about it, so excited he could barely sleep.

He would wake up in middle of the night and just start writing. Thoughts and ideas would just come to him out of nowhere. He knew it had to be God working because he never graduated school, there's no way he could create some of the things he came up with on his own.

Or maybe he was smart the whole time but by following the wrong people all his life he always did what they did, so he never had to use that part of his brain.

Anyway whatever it was and wherever it came from, it didn't show up until he decided to tag team with God.

He felt unstoppable like he could do anything in the world. His faith became greater, his trust in God became stronger and his love, well let's just say that if Erica wasn't already pregnant she would be.

A spirit of love came over JB, he started showing love to everybody, especially Erica. He loved her even more than the day he said *I do*.

He thought about one of the conversations he and Mr. Trudi had back in prison. The one about how do you know when you're a Christian. At that very moment is when he knew he no longer had to ask that question anymore.

He had made a total 180 change.

He didn't look the same, act the same, talk the same or think the same.

Then all of a sudden something popped up in his head. Where in the world could his Dad be? What would he think of the man his son had become? He knew nothing about his father. The only way he even knew what he looked like was from the handful of pictures his mom kept over the years.

*He wondered, was his dad a Christian? Was he a drunk? Was he a police officer? Was he a drug dealer? Was he in prison? Was he married? Did he have other children? And most of all, Was he even still alive?*

He did something he never thought about doing before, he called a private investigator to find out how much it would cost to locate his father.

Next he prayed on it and asked God for strength to forgive his dad for never being there. He wasn't even sure that if he found his father whether he would get along with him. Would that awkward feeling be there or would they laughed and talk as if he was always in JB's life?

JB had always wanted to know his father, however, he did not know if his father wanted to know him. If he did, why didn't he ever try to look for him?

JB felt himself becoming angry so he quickly occupied his mind with something else. He opened his Bible to his favorite scripture: *Psalm 37:4: "Delight yourself also in the Lord and he shall give you the desires of your heart."*

It was his favorite because he found it to be faithful during his life. It also was his favorite because it was the very first Scripture he learned when he began his walk with God. Speaking of walk with God, JB also remembered that Mr. Trudi said it was going to be the hardest thing he ever had to do.

He thought he must have been lucky because he skipped right past the hard part.

He saw his walk as easy, what was hard about helping people and doing the right thing? What was hard about being happy and feeling that feeling of freedom? What Mr. Trudi probably meant was that it was hard for those individuals who were unsure of what they wanted; difficult for people that didn't want to let go of their worldly life and choices.

He didn't have that problem, for him walking away from the streets was just as simple as walking down the street.

Sure he missed the fun but the one thing that came with the fun was the trouble and he didn't miss that at all. He didn't care if people called him *soft* (which they did), *church boy* (which they did), *sprung* and a lot of other names. He didn't allow things like that to get under his skin.

They couldn't see that he changed his lifestyle for the better. The smiles instead of headaches, the weight lifted from not having to look over your shoulder every twenty seconds.

The turned-up party-goer turned party-pooper.

They saw the six or seven grand a week drug dealer with lots of women, fancy cars, and beautiful houses trade all that for a $500 to $600 per week construction job, one wife, a cheap car that barely ran, and a two bedroom apartment.

In their eyes he was about as stupid as they come.

However, in God's eyes he was a faithful child living right; an heir ready to receive life more abundantly and inherit all the riches of the kingdom of heaven.

So, He couldn't care less about what anyone thought. If they knew half of what they thought they knew they would jump on board the train. Because the truth was that JB was going places.

He was now walking with God.

# CHAPTER 10

———‹◇›———

JB didn't feel held down by the Devil anymore. Even when he was a big time drug dealer he knew he could only go so far. You can only take over so much of the city before you are stepping on someone else's toes, then it becomes a war. Or you could only sell so much before they stopped releasing you from jail and keep you for life.

You can only survive so long until eventually it all comes to an end... and it always comes to end.

There's probably not a drug dealer in history that sold his or her whole life and went untouched, it just doesn't happen that way. But walking with God was the total opposite. There was no limit; people say that the sky's the limit but heaven is beyond that so really there is no limit.

JB could praise the Lord until his last breath, worship until his heart stopped and there was nothing nobody could do about it, not even the devil.

He could go as high as God could take him and never come down if he chose not to. The chains that were holding him were broken, the only person that could bound him up again was himself.

Therefore, when his wife asked him, *Baby where do you see us in 5 years from now?* he responded, "Well I feel like the chains are finally broken, so with God's help we can be in a beautiful big house with Mercy running around playing. I know you gonna be a lawyer, and I should have the Detour Foundation up and running.

Oh, baby I see us nowhere close to where we are now. I see us playing a significant role in the community; I see my name and picture on billboards on the side of the interstate. I see an overflow of blessings showering down from heaven.

The devil won't know what hit him, he won't know how to come at us. Everything he does will get shut down. God's mighty hand will be on us, His shield of protection will keep us safe. Favor will follow you in the courtroom; you will win every case even the hardest cases."

Before Erica knew it the Holy Spirit had taken over him. He was prophesying without even knowing.

She said, "Baby you forgot one thing."

"What's that?"

Erica said in a joking way, "You going to be a preacher."

"Oh, Naw I ain't trying to do all that."

"Well that's what you was just doing. If I wouldn't have stopped you we would probably be having church up in here, Amen Pastor Griffin."

He chuckled and said, "Okay... you got jokes."

"I'm just saying you never know what the LORD might have in store for you. Just like you never thought you would be right here with me."

"Yeah... I definitely ain't think I was going to be married to you, I ain't think I was gone be married at all."

*He paused briefly.*

"I ain't think my best friend would turn on me and try to get me locked up either."

"Yep, our whole life we believe something is one way not knowing that God already designed our life to be another way."

"Right...we never know, just like you don't know what I'm thinking right now?"

"What are you thinking Jonathan?"

"Right now I'm thinking why the heck did my momma name me Jonathan? And you love to say it too; I'm gone change it so you can't call me that. My new name is Steve."

"Now I know you playing now. I won't ever call you Steve, I rather call you Gary before I call you Steve. You don't even look like a Steve."

"I sho don't look like a Gary either."

"Naw I'm just playing but for real guess what I'm thinking."

"I don't know baby what, you want me to go cook?"

'Yes you can 'Cause I'm hungry but nope that's not it."

"I give up I don't know what you thinking. But I'm thinking I wish you hurry up and tell me because I'm hungry too."

"I'm thinking all this was just a test maybe. Just to see if I pass and go to the next level. If I would've failed I probably would have ended up like Mike or like Chris. And my momma too, I know she prayed and she had lots of other people praying for her but I feel like, well I'm not saying my prayer is the one that took the cancer away but I feel like I was connected a little bit to that.

Like if I was responsible for her having a heart attack then maybe her cancer had something to do with me too. Like if I would've still been on the streets she wouldn't be here, but since I gave my life to Christ, he saved her.

I don't really know how to put it."

"I see what you mean baby."

"I don't know, maybe I'm just being selfish but sometimes I be thinking crazy like that. So I'm just glad I did, and I'm pleased that I have a Father like Him that would still love me after everything I did. I'm glad he sent an angel to work at Starbucks. If you would have took off that day I might not be here. So I think you are an angel."

"Aww baby that was so sweet, I love you."

"I love you too now get in that kitchen fat belly."

"Shut up you made it like that."

"Yep and when you drop that one, I'm gone blow it up again. Gotta sow a lot of seeds to get a big harvest right?"

"Not that many, I don't know who you think fenna be running behind all them Lil' hard headed Rugrats."

"My kid's ain't gone be no Rugrats, they gone be baby geniuses."

JB remembered what his mom told him about generational curses. How her and his dad's life and the way they lived, the things they did, might have played a part in his life. It was possible that all the problems he went through and situations he had to face was nothing more than him paying the price for the mistakes they made in their lives and their parents before them.

It was written in the Bible that God placed curses on whole blood lines for things one person did wrong. All he was hoping was that he had finally broken that curse if there was one. He didn't want his kids to have to suffer for nothing he had done.

**\* \* \***

A couple more weeks went by and Erica had not worked because she was on maternity leave. She stayed around the house as much as she could, but she wasn't the 'lay' around type. She couldn't stand lying in bed watching TV all day. That drove her crazy. If she wasn't at home she was either in two places; her mom's house or JB's mom's house.

JB went to work every day but he kept his phone close because any day could be the baby day.

He was anxious in every way. He couldn't wait to see his baby boy. He wrecked his brain every day thinking so much about who the baby would look like... *How tall will he be? How much will he weigh? Is he going to come in the morning or at night?*

Even though they had everything they could possibly have for a newborn he still felt like he was missing something. Then he thought about it, he wasn't missing anything he had everything he needed, he had GOD. Then he started thinking maybe that was why he lost his twins in the past, because he didn't have God. He wasn't ready for kids then but now things were better in his life, his life was set up for success.

The book was coming along good even though he was still only in the first chapter. His business plan for The Detour Foundation was just about complete. He wasn't rushing it because he wanted it to be perfect, that way the government would be stupid not to give him the funds to start it.

He prayed and asked GOD to give him the vision to make his foundation stand out from all the rest. He didn't want to just tell youngsters that there was another way besides the streets, he wanted to show them.

His mom always said, *"No one is going to hold your hand. You have to do it on your own."*

JB decided to go against that saying.

His foundation was going to be the one that held a kid's hand to help them every step of the way. He was determined to show them they wouldn't have to do it on their own.

Other programs just tutor kids, help them with their homework and watch them after school like a babysitting service. Homework and babysitting was nowhere in JB's plans. His vision was more on the lines of a Military Academy, training you to go to war against this streets.

Say no to drugs, say no to crime and basically say no to anything that is not of God.

He knew that the negative things that were going on in the world were being passed down to each generation. Like a torch, the old heads training and passing it on to the young heads. If he could find a way to get a whole generation to refuse to take the torch then it wouldn't get passed, so it would have no choice but to die.

That's when he came up with his first assignment as the CEO of The Detour Foundation. Once up and running he would launch the *Past the Torch Project*. If there was going to be a torch passed it was going to be a positive one. Somewhere somehow kids and teens found it to be cool to get in trouble. It was time to reverse that thought and create a new one.

*If we all learn to get along with each other, then we wouldn't fight, and the chains would be broken.*

*If we all refused to bring harm to one another, then there would be killings, and the chains would be broken.*

*If we all refused to commit crimes, jails and prisons wouldn't fill up, and the chains would be broken*

*If we all refused to sell drugs, then the drug dealers will eventually fade away, and the chains would be broken*

*If we all refused to do drugs, there would be no need for them, and the chains would be broken.*

*If we all refuse to give into the devil, then he loses every battle, and the chains will be broken.*

*If we all love our neighbors as we love ourselves, then every chain will be broken.*

*If we all turned from our wicked ways and followed our Lord Jesus Christ, then the chains will be broken.*

JB was really onto something.

If he could pull off just half of what he thought, it would kick off the biggest thing that ever happened in his city.

He thought, if he could somehow do like the Salvation Army, Goodwill or Boys & Girls Club and get The Detour Foundation stationed in every city across America then it could quickly turn into the largest movement for improvement in the world today.

JB was feeling so pumped up that if the devil were here on earth he would walk right up to him and Mike Tyson punch him in the face.

More and more each day JB became in tune with his spiritual side. Even though he still listened to a little Hip Hop now and then he left the hard-core gangsta rap alone. If it wasn't positive, he didn't listen to it.

Well, he and Erica still played a few slow jams in the bedroom, but that was different.

He no longer celebrated Halloween either, when that day came around he and Erica did not put up decorations or pass out candy.

They stopped watching horror films because they represented evil. He tried carefully to make sure that every move he made was in a direction that was pleasing to God. He wasn't perfect, he still had flaws but he wanted to please God. So every day that's what he worked on; striving to be a better man to ensure a more stable life for his family.

It was time; Erica's water broke while JB was out at the store. Interrupting his train of thought... the phone rang ...

*Ring ... ring ... ring*

JB answered the phone to hear Erica yelling on the other end.

"Yes baby..."

She yelled, *"I'm having the baby hurry up."*

JB left what he had in his hand and ran out of the store. "Hold on baby... don't have it yet I'm three minutes away, what are you doing right now?"

*"I just told you I'm having the baby."* She screamed, *"JB, I am hurting!"*

"I'm right around the corner... baby you not having the baby in the house, are you?"

"I don't know, it feels like he's coming right now."

"No not in the house we gotta get you to the hospital, can you make it outside?"

"I don't know I'm on the couch."

"Okay honey... just stay there I'm pulling up in the driveway now." JB whipped up in front of the house and threw the car in park. He ran into the house, grabbed the baby bag, and his wife and slowly guided her out of the house to the car. He rushed to the hospital as quickly and safely as he could.

Erica must have been right about the baby coming because she was only in labor for twenty-five minutes.

As soon as the doctor laid her on the bed and saw how many centimeters she had dilated, he started getting ready for the delivery process

The doctor stated, "Looks like this little one wants out. Is this your first child ma'am?"

"Yes"

"Well get ready to be a mother very soon. Now relax… everything will be okay."

JB looked at Erica and said, "yes, baby, it's finally happening." He had the biggest and happiest smile on his face. Erica was happy too but she wasn't smiling though; she was in pain and ready for it to be over.

Before long, baby Mercy was born 8 lbs. 3 oz. at 6:17 pm on a Wednesday night. He was a beautiful boy, a miracle blessing from God.

The couple was as happy as can be.

JB's Aunt Janice picked up Cynthia, and they came down to the hospital. Erica's mom showed up ten minutes after.

The family gathered around, talking and laughing. The pastor even came and said a sweet prayer welcoming the baby into the world. He prayed a covering over the couple and their new child, then a separate one for the family as a whole.

The Holy Spirit filled the hospital that night.

Two days later Erica was released, and they took their baby home. JB returned to work on Monday while Erica stayed at home resting and learning how to be a mom.

JB couldn't believe how well his wife was doing and how well things were going. JB thought back to when everything all around him was crumbling; how it looked like the hood was all he was ever going to know.

Just when it looked like JB's life was all coming to an end, it was just getting started. He thanked God over and over again because he knew that anything was possible. He was aware that it was never too late.

He was mindful of the fact that the only way to get something different was to try something different.

He knew that the chains were broken.

After he finished work he called his wife. "Baby are you alright? How's Mercy?"

"Yes, I'm okay baby, he just laying right here sleep. Are you off yet?"

"Yep, I'm on the way home now I was just checking on ya'll."

"Okay, see you when you get here." "Okay, love you."

"I love you too."

When JB pulled up in the driveway someone was sitting on his front porch waiting for him, it was *Can Man*. He served thirty days in jail for an open container, public intoxication and disturbing the peace.

However, he was free and ready to talk.

He walked over to JB's car just as JB was getting out, "*Can Man* ... what's up buddy? Man I ain't seen you in a while. I didn't know what happened to you. I see you got on the shoes I gave you. So how are you doing? You ready to talk?"

"Yep, that's why I'm here."

JB looked up to the sky and said, "Thank you, Jesus." He looked back at *Can Man*, he put one hand on his shoulder and said, "Step into my office."

To Be Continued . . .

# ABOUT THE AUTHOR

———◇———

Rashard "Brother Rizz" Royster is indeed a humble, intelligent, creative man who is motivated from his past experiences. Working hard to achieve greatness has always been his number one goal. Born on August 14, 1980 in St. Petersburg, FL many people place caps on how far they believe young African American males from such an area will go.

He currently resides in Lithonia, GA. His relationship with God is the most important thing in life, and he sets out to spread the love of Christ.

Growing up, Rashard has been a victim to various struggles and seeing his mother go through domestic violence made a major impact on his behavior; which led him into alcohol and drug addiction, multiple encounters with the law, being a high school dropout, and living a very unstable lifestyle. Rashard finds writing and recording music therapeutic for him; which is one of the main reasons he began writing a book in hopes to help someone that is going through similar struggles. In the meantime, Rashard plans to write more books, changing lives, recording music, and being the best servant and father, he can be.

Visit the Author at: **Facebook: BrokenC**